# HONEYMOON FOR ONE

# HONEYMOON FOR ONE

HONEYMOON SERIES, BOOK 1

LILY ZANTE

# AUTHOR'S NOTE

'*Honeymoon For One*' is the first book in the '*Honeymoon Series*' and tells the story of a bride jilted weeks before her Valentine's Day wedding. This is the first of a five-part series based around the same couple.

I have also written a spin-off series called the '*Italian Summer Series*' which tells the stories of some of the minor characters who first appeared in the '*Honeymoon Series*'.

The timelines of both series are connected and you can find a recommended reading order here.

**Honeymoon Series:**

**Italian Summer Series:**

(A spin-off from the Honeymoon Series)

It Takes Two
All That Glitters
Fool's Gold
Roman Encounter
November Sun
New Beginnings
Italian Summer Series (Books 1-4)

# CHAPTER ONE

Ava lay on the couch and wiped her raw nose again. Her head throbbed with shooting pain and she wanted to close her eyes and drift off to sleep, but she couldn't. Damn this flu.

Connor would be here soon, she thought, with some consolation. Wincing in pain, she blew her nose yet again and sank back onto the couch, dragging the chenille blanket up to her neck.

Swatches of peach-colored organza and pale pink silk fabric lay on the side at her feet. As soon as her mind cleared enough she would choose one fabric and this would signal the start of the wedding favors sub-project. For now she was too congested to think straight.

Wearily she grabbed the television control. *When Harry Met Sally* was on and she flicked back and forth between live coverage of the New Year's Eve celebrations in Times Square and the romantic film she had seen countless times. It was 11:14 p.m.

*Connor will be here soon. What's keeping him so long?*

The loud cheers on TV woke her up. The Robitussin had done its job and she had managed to slip into a delicious sleep. Ava shook her head, not quite believing the clock on the television screen. It was midnight already. A digital counter in one corner of the screen counted down, "10... 9...8...7..."

No sign of Connor anywhere.

She grabbed her cell and called him, her heart racing with thoughts of anything and everything that could have gone wrong.

*Dear god, not now.*

"5...4..."

"Connor? Where are you? I've been worried sick." A part of her was relieved to hear his voice again and to know that he was all right, and another part of her was angry that he wasn't by her side on this special night.

"3...2...1...Happy New Year, everybody!" The crowds went crazy in the main square and New Year's Eve confetti rained down from the skies.

It was here. The New Year had finally arrived. And the wedding was only six weeks away. A burst of happiness exploded through her, wiping out the worry she had felt when Connor hadn't turned up.

"Happy New Year, darling." She smiled as she said it, even though her head hurt and her throat felt as though it had been sandpapered.

There was a pause at the other end.

"I can't do it, Ava. I'm sorry." Connor sounded dull and quiet, but in the background she could hear everyone at Russell's house party screaming and hooting for joy.

She blinked in confusion. Had she heard him right? Maybe the Robitussen was playing tricks on her.

"Can't do what, Connor?" she asked in a muffled voice, as she wiped her nose with a soggy Kleenex.

"I can't marry you. I'm sorry. I can't go through with it." His words cut her more than her throbbing headache or throat.

"What? Connor?" *What did you just say?*

"I'm sorry, I can't go through with the wedding. I don't think I love you."

She had heard him the first time.

*I don't think I love you.*

From deep inside her, she managed to find the strength to say, "You don't?" but it was more to herself, than to him, and then she hung up. She felt as though she was back in high school, tall, gangly, big-eyed, and long-necked and the coolest girls in school picked on her for looking like a freak. Then as now, she felt her body shaking all over, except that it didn't really feel as though she was inside it. The next moment she collapsed backwards onto the couch and let out a gut wrenching scream, flinging her arms out and sending the swatches of organza and silk fabric hovering delicately to the floor. She heard a primal, guttural sound ringing in the air and it took her a few seconds to figure out that it was her voice.

*I don't think I love you.*

Their wedding was only six weeks away.

On TV the crowds hugged and kissed one another, and the euphoric partygoers were all smiles and laughter. They had high hopes for this new start to a new year. Sick at the sight of so much happiness, Ava smacked the TV off and curled up into a ball. She hid under the soft comfort of the blanket.

A short while later Ava woke up and found herself

staring at the ceiling. She had dozed off with the light on and even now, hovering on the edge of sleep and wakefulness, the first words she remembered were Connor's.

*I don't think I love you.*

The words punctured her like knife wounds. She loved him, and he loved her. He *had* loved her. She shuddered, still unable to grasp the finality of his words. What had happened? Where was he now? Did she really even know for sure?

She needed more Robitussen; her headache was back and the shivers had started up again. She'd thought she was getting better. Getting over it. And now she had something much bigger to get over, not just a fever.

She lay on the couch, sniffling into her Kleenex, her mind a whirlwind of despair, she kept thinking back to the past few months. They hadn't been all warm and happy. They'd had constant rows, many to do with the wedding preparations. But sometimes more to do with Connor's work, the fact that he'd be away when she needed him at weekends to finalize the flower arrangements, or to design the cake. Other wedding things he had effectively managed to dodge.

Why hadn't she seen the warning signs then? They seemed so clear now that she looked back, with the great gift of hindsight.

Because even though they had been together for nearly three years, if Ava really analyzed their relationship, she and Connor had started to drift apart during the last six months.

These had been defining times for their relationship, and deep in her very core her soul had known that somehow, maybe, something wasn't quite right.

She had seen Connor become something that he had never been in all the time she had known him: distant. And the distance had increased the closer the wedding date loomed.

Now with only six weeks to go, maybe the pressure had gotten too much. Maybe it was her doing? She pushed him too much? After all, he was a corporate lawyer and he had great demands. Had she driven him to this?

Ava blew her nose again and briefly wondered whether she should go and sleep in her bedroom. It was such a trivial thing to think about; there was comfort in thinking about small things. But she couldn't summon the willpower to move her body.

Instead, she closed her eyes.

# CHAPTER TWO

The next morning Ava woke up in an awkward position with a dull ache on the left side of her body. She had slept badly on the couch and this morning she was paying the price for neglecting her bed.

She sat up on the couch and reached over to the floor for her cell phone. Everything she needed was on there and she always checked her emails, messages, calendar, and to-do list for the day before taking a single step out of bed. It always gave her a great kick to check her sales figures for her small, but thriving, online store for kids. Soon, she hoped, she wouldn't even need to do any copywriting work to help pay the bills.

This morning an email from Connor grabbed her attention first. She noted the time of the email; he had sent it at a quarter to four in the morning.

*Dear Ava*

. . .

*S*orry I broke the news to you as I did yesterday, just on the stroke of midnight. You deserve better than that. I'm sorry.

I don't feel I can carry on. I think I love you, but sometimes I'm not sure I do. The thought of marriage scares the hell out of me. I'm not sure I'm the marrying type. Everything was great between us. But as you got more carried away with everything for the big day, I got more and more frightened by the sense of responsibility. You talked about babies and I'm still thinking about my career. Babies weren't in my career plan. But they are in yours. I can't take that away from you.

It wasn't just that. I knew I couldn't go through with the wedding and I owe it to you to tell you this. That weekend I told you I went to a law seminar in Connecticut. I did. But I also ended up sleeping with a woman I met from another law firm. I knew then that if I was capable of that, the one thing I wasn't going to do was to let you think marriage to me was the way forward. I hope you'll find it in your heart to forgive me one day.

*Connor.*

It hadn't been a dream after all.

She dropped the cell phone on the floor and buried her face in her hands. But the tears did not come. The course of her whole life ahead had changed and she was too numb to feel a thing.

Paralyzed, she sat frozen on the couch, her mind vaguely working out that there would be no need to panic over wedding favors fabric anymore. With a sinking heart she realized that her mother had invited her and Connor over for a late lunch today. Her mother had also invited her other daughter, her son-in-law, and of course, little Tori too.

*Great.*

A family get together on today of all days.

The thought of seeing her closest family and breaking this news to them filled her with dread. But she had to start somewhere.

———

E lsa Ramirez lived alone in Cherry Creek, a small suburb within the Denver city limits. She had invited her daughter and future son-in-law over for lunch on New Year's Day.

A widowed woman, in her late sixties, Elsa was a social butterfly with a full and busy social life. Yet she always made time to see her two daughters, Ava and Rona.

She wasn't too worried about Rona. Rona's husband, Carlos, looked after her well, and she was busy enjoying life as a new mother to six-month-old Tori.

It was Ava that she was more concerned about. This wedding was taking its toll on her daughter; she could see that. Her daughter was busy enough as it was, what with her copywriting assignments and her online store, and now the wedding preparations had taken over.

Each day she hoped the final arrangements for the wedding would be drawing near, but each time her perfectionist daughter would go the extra mile doing everything to make the big day extra special. The wedding preparations were never ending.

Elsa sniffed in annoyance as she peeled the potatoes and diced the cabbage, checking the ham steak every now and then.

She would put up with Connor for the sake of her daughter, but, Elsa thought, ferociously dicing the cabbage for the sauerkraut, she didn't feel completely at ease around him.

Not that it would matter now. She would have to keep her mouth tightly closed because Ava was happy. This was all that mattered. Still, she would keep her eyes open and watch Connor closely.

She sensed that her daughter always tried to live up to what she perceived to be Connor's ideals. His family were rich, and he came from a long line of lawyers. Elsa had met Connor's parents once. They were all cold smiles and eyes that gave away no expression. It was clear that they had met and liked Ava on a number of occasions. But Elsa wasn't convinced that his parents thought Ava was good enough stock for their son. Not to marry.

With six weeks until the wedding day, Elsa hoped everything would go according to plan. She prayed her daughter would be happy and that her future son-in-law would be good to her.

She opened the oven door and checked the ham steak. It looked just perfect.

---

The ham steak was cooked to perfection and on a normal day Ava would have had a second helping. As it was, she was having problems getting down her first few bites.

When she couldn't stand it any longer, she put down her cutlery and looked for the right time to do it.

"I have something to say," she announced. Her heart thumped and the back of her throat pulsated when her mother and sister looked up sharply from their food.

Carlos chewed impassively and only a sharp dig in the ribs from Rona made him sit up and pay attention.

"The wedding's off." Ava's flat voice was devoid of any emotion.

Carlos stopped chewing for a few seconds. Rona said, "What?" then "Are you sure?"

Only her mother remained silent. But Ava felt her mother's stare penetrating her soul.

"I'm sure." Ava reached out for a glass of water, wanting the moment over, fast.

"What happened? What do you mean it's off?" Rona threw down her napkin. Beside her, Carlos's fork slipped and landed on his plate with a nervous clatter.

"He says he can't go through with it and that he's sorry." Ava stared at them with her gray-blue eyes that now showed signs of a tearful night.

She swallowed some water. Her throat was parched and although her fever had gone, she now felt her face getting hot again. The dark circles under her eyes gave her face a sunken appearance.

In the background, they heard the stirring noises of a baby's cry. With her attention firmly on Ava, Rona ignored her baby's cries. "But the wedding's six weeks away!" Rona gasped.

"Not any more. There's not going to be a wedding. Can we please not talk about it?" Ava was calm, but inside her chest tightened. She wanted to go home.

"Why's it taken him so long to realize? Are you sure it's not just nerves? A lot of men go through that," Rona suggested.

"Carlos didn't." Ava played with her food.

"I wouldn't dare," Carlos muttered under his breath.

Tori's crying turned louder still.

"Will you go and check on the baby, for chrissakes!"

hissed Rona. Reluctantly, Carlos put his fork down and got up.

Ava felt the heat of her mother's stare on her face. She avoided meeting her gaze.

"Are you sure this is final, Ava?" Elsa asked, reaching out and clasping her daughter's hand in hers.

Although he had broken her heart, telling her family was akin to twisting the blade in further. The love and concern of her immediate family saddened her. "He said he's not the marrying type, Mom. He said wedding talk scared him. It scared him so much he slept with another woman a few weeks ago." She was bone weary and dog tired. Her aching muscles craved a soft bed and all night slumber.

Elsa put her hand to her mouth.

Rona and Carlos gasped together.

And the baby started crying louder than ever.

"Better that you found out now, my love." Elsa squeezed her daughter's hand even tighter.

Rona got up and snatched the baby from Carlos, then walked over to Ava with Tori balanced precariously on her hip. She kissed Ava on the head lightly.

"He doesn't deserve you."

*Sisters would say that.* Ava was miserable. The truth of it was that she missed Connor. He should have been sitting here beside her. He should have been a part of this family meal. He would have been joining her family and soon they would have been a married couple. But now all of those dreams had disappeared.

"Are you sure it's not just a misunderstanding, Ava? Something about him getting cold feet? Can this be sorted out?"

Ava shook her head. No. There was nothing to be sorted

out here. It had happened and Connor didn't love her. When had he stopped loving her, she wondered?

Could it be that Connor wasn't just getting cold feet now. Could it be that his feet had never been firmly there in the first place?

## CHAPTER THREE

It was Valentine's Day and it should have been the day of Ava's wedding.

Instead, Rona had come over with Tori to help her clear up her apartment. Ava knew neither her mother nor her sister had wanted her to spend the day alone.

What Rona didn't know was that Ava had been busy packing for her solo honeymoon.

Ever since their breakup, Ava had busied herself with wedding preparations once more, except that this time she cancelled everything. All the suppliers, dressmakers, caterers, and party planners had been informed and all the money had been refunded, minus the cancellation costs.

When Rona had come over this morning, Ava had just returned from her five-mile run. It always cleared her head. The time was right to tell Rona of her decision.

"You're doing *what?*" Baby Tori was spitting drool all over her shoulder as Rona faced Ava with the baby on one hip, performing a fine balancing act in the process.

"I'm going on my honeymoon," countered Ava. She

sauntered around the room in her tracksuit pants. Her hair was untidily thrown up into a high ponytail.

"But you cancelled everything."

"No," said Ava, "*You* cancelled the hotel, the caterers and everything else. *I've* been dealing with the honeymoon and bridesmaids' and wedding dresses."

"And you *didn't* cancel the honeymoon?" Rona stared at her younger sister in utter bewilderment. "Let me guess. Mom knows about this too, right?"

Ava nodded, unable to stop herself as she burst out laughing. The look of horror on her sister's face was priceless.

"So let me get this straight," said Rona, drool stained her yellow T-shirt as she walked around with a white muslin square in her hand. "Mom's happy for you to go?"

Ava nodded. "She thinks it's a great idea." Ava sat on the floor and untied her shoelaces. She remembered her mother's reaction when she told her what she was planning on doing.

*"Go, Ava, go and enjoy yourself and forget all about this mess here. Sometimes things look bleak just before you hit the peaks. Go."*

Her mother had been instrumental in helping Ava get over the shock of what Connor had done. Yet she'd always had a feeling that her mother wasn't really too fond of Connor anyway.

Ava sighed, letting the big smile on her face grow wider as she looked up at her sister. It was obvious Rona didn't like the idea one bit.

"Let me get this straight. We've been cancelling all things wedding related for the past month, right?" asked Rona, wiping Tori's face.

Ava nodded.

"And now you tell me that everything's done, cancelled, finished, ended, *except* for the honeymoon?" The muslin square dangled furiously in her hand as she gesticulated at full speed.

Ava nodded again.

"But you have this insane idea of going to Italy anyway? Alone?" The muslin square came to a complete standstill.

Ava nodded.

"Does Connor know?"

Ava's insides hardened. "Why should he? He's not in my life anymore. He dumped me, remember?"

"Right." Rona backed off. Ava could tell that her sister clearly thought she was crazy.

She pulled off her sneakers and sat with her back flat against the wall. Her morning run had done its usual wonders for her mind and body. When she ran, the blood flushed through her veins, her lungs fought for air, and her muscles strained to go the distance. All of these things made her feel alive and free.

It was also on her runs that she thought about Connor and tried to sift through the debris of their relationship. She tried to recall their time together so that she could figure out when everything had started to go wrong.

She'd loved him.

*And she still did.*

A piece of her shredded heart found it hard to let go of him completely.

It wasn't just that he had dumped her so cruelly, but admitting that he had slept with a woman at the convention had given her sleepless nights, too.

He'd been away so often and to so many law seminars and courses this past year that she was now starting to wonder if he'd been cheating on her a lot longer than he'd owned up to.

For Ava, Connor had been everything. But he'd crushed her to pieces and she now found herself examining every area of their life together in order to sift through what was real and what was not.

Trust and loyalty were a huge part of who she was. She had never so much as looked at another man, even though many of her friends' boyfriends had always been too eager to strike up a conversation with her whenever she'd met them.

Connor had been part of her world; a comfortable and constant little world in which she worked on her copywriting projects during the day and slaved over her online store until the early hours of the morning.

Now as surely as he'd thrown a grenade between them, he had blasted their relationship, and in the process, her life, to pieces.

She would never trust him again.

She didn't think she'd ever be able to trust *any* man again.

Two years from thirty, she now had to face facts. It was time to move on. She had to make something of her life instead of wallowing in self-pity.

After all, Connor seemed to be moving forward with his life with no regard for her.

Growing her online store was the new big goal in her life this year.

"When are you going?"

"Tomorrow," she replied calmly and waited for her sister's outburst.

"Tomorrow?" Rona shrieked. "And you waited until the last minute to tell me?"

Ava nodded apologetically. "I didn't mean to hold out on you, but if I'd told you any sooner, you would've tried to talk me out of it."

"What exactly do you propose to do out there all on your own?" asked Rona, not without a touch of malice in her voice as she placed Tori on the floor. She carefully wiped the drool from her mouth.

"Enjoy myself?" replied Ava cheekily. "You know, Rona, maybe I don't need to have a man around me to feel validated." She rubbed her aching feet with her slender fingers.

"That may be, but this man who *validated* you," Rona mimicked Ava's words, "was with you for three years." There was a hint of sarcasm in her voice before she softened her tone a little. "Look, I'm glad he's out of your life. I'm glad that the one decent thing he did after he ditched you was to tell you about that whore he slept with."

"She wasn't a whore. She was a woman from another firm."

"Right." The sarcasm was hard to miss. Rona walked around, picking Tori's things up off the floor. "And now she's your best friend all of a sudden."

"She might not have known that he was engaged."

Rona rolled her eyes in disbelief. "Like that would have made any difference."

"She might have done me a favor," said Ava hotly, her face was glowing and she needed to take a shower. In actual fact, she needed Rona out of her apartment because she needed time alone to think.

"How's that?" Rona stopped and waited for an answer with a baby rattle in her hand.

"Maybe things between us wouldn't have worked out in the end. Maybe I got too carried away with the wedding and it scared him. I feel as though we'd been walking different paths lately anyway. Maybe him ending up with her was his way of bailing out of us."

"Maybe he could have told you instead of sleeping with

her. Maybe, maybe, maybe." Rona shook her head in annoyance. "You should listen to yourself sometimes."

Ava ignored her. "Connor wasn't ready and I was up to my eyeballs in pink organza wedding favors. Maybe it was all my fault. I should have been less pushy about the wedding instead of being so obsessed by it all." She pulled her knees up and hugged her arms around them. "What if Connor didn't really love me at all?"

Rona slid down on the floor next to Ava and tapped her on the knee with the baby rattle. "I don't know what went on in that man's head, so I can't tell you the answer to that. But, like you said, maybe this holiday will do you some good. Take time out and clear your head." Rona leaned her head against Ava's and they sat quietly for a few moments while Tori gurgled happily on the floor. "I still think it's a stupid idea though."

There was only one thing left to do and Ava didn't want to do it.

She didn't want to face Connor now. Especially not just before she was going away.

Soon after the split she had hoped that they could have met and talked things through. But he'd only ever called her once and texted her a couple of times and that had been nearly three weeks *after* the split. She had desperately wanted to know what it was that put him off her; so that she would know how to change herself for next time. He'd made no moves to meet up. Hadn't seemed remotely interested. It was odd, strange behavior and she was at a loss. They hadn't seen each other since he'd left her, ill at home on New Year's Eve, while he went to a friend's party.

Most definitely, the time for talking had long gone. The way she saw things, she was setting off on a new adventure in her life. It was a chance to look forward, not back. It was her opportunity to forge an independent future for herself. And being her own boss was a big part of that.

Romance was not a part of this new future. She had a lot to learn about men, and beginning to trust them was like taking a huge step into the unknown. It was something she wasn't ready for now, and she wasn't sure she would be, ever.

"Just be careful. And promise me one thing?"

Ava shrugged and wondered what her sister was going to make her promise. Rona got up and gathered all of the baby's toys into her baby bag. "If you insist on taking this trip, don't go around feeling sad and hopeless 'cause of all the shit you've just been through."

Ava scowled at her sister.

Rona carried on regardless. "I've heard that in Italy the men are hot blooded. You with your long dark hair and dazzling gray eyes are going to attract a lot of attention, especially going alone and all that. I know what you're like; you'll get there and have no thought for your own safety. Promise me that you'll at least wear your wedding band."

"I don't have a wedding band. Remember? We didn't quite make it to the altar."

"Take one of mine. It's not my wedding ring, but it'll do. It's the least you can do for me." Rona twisted off one of the many rings she wore on her fingers and handed Ava a plain one. "Here. It'll keep you safe from the men who'll hassle you if they think you're single. And don't go flying into the arms of any tall, dark and handsome Italians either. Don't tell them your sob story."

"You must think I was born yesterday. Give me a break, Rona. I'm not stupid." She got up off the floor and faced Rona with her hands on her hips. "Anyway, how's wearing this ring going to help?" She squinted at it suspiciously.

"They'll think you're married and leave you alone."

Ava stifled a laugh. "Are you serious?"

"Of course. *Someone* has to be."

Ava shook her head. "You're impossible. And impossibly silly, too."

"I love you and I want you to be safe."

"I'm going to have a ball on this trip." Ava walked over to her bag and extracted something from her purse. "I'll wear your fake wedding ring if you promise me that you'll hand deliver this to Connor." She held out the 1.2-carat engagement ring he had given her.

"Can't I just wear this for a few weeks first?" Rona's eyes widened when she slipped the ring onto her fingers and flashed her hand around, admiring the way the light glinted off its facets as it sparkled brilliantly.

"Do what you want with it." Ava had no interest in the thing. She picked up the baby and hugged her to her chest, then swung around with her. Tori gurgled, enjoying the motion.

"Look after your crazy mom for me will you, Tori? And make sure she returns that ring after I've left. And don't tell Connor where I've gone either." She handed Tori back to Rona.

"I'll return it to him, once you're safely on your way to Italy, I promise. But don't you think you should at least meet once face-to-face?"

"He hadn't shown any interest in meeting me. He texted once to ask if I was okay. I replied, asking if he wanted to talk things through. He never got back to me. Connor doesn't care about me."

Rona shook her head, gave Ava an apologetic look. "I didn't realize he was such a jackass."

"He wasn't always like this," said Ava in a quiet voice. But she had nothing else to say.

Rona gave her sister a big hug. "You take care of you, okay?"

Ava nodded and managed a weak smile.

After Rona left, Ava started packing her suitcase. She would travel light. She packed a couple of dresses but mainly jeans and tops. She closed her small suitcase, got her hand luggage ready, and prepared for an early night. She had said her goodbyes to her family earlier in the day.

Tomorrow she would be setting off on her little adventure and leaving Denver for Rome.

# CHAPTER FOUR

—————————

Ava stared at her reflection in the starkly lit mirror inside the crowded cubicle of a toilet.

She looked a complete mess: her large puffy eyes had dark shadows smudged underneath. She closed her eyes and splashed cold water over her face. Then, as the plane tanked a little from slight turbulence, half of the water went all over her shirt; the sudden shock of the cold made her gasp.

Patting her face dry with a small tissue, she stared in the mirror—as much as she could without swaying from side to side. She couldn't even brush her hair properly. With her throat parched, Ava coughed roughly and swept back her long, brown hair away from her forehead.

She had been awake for nearly twenty-four hours, unable to sleep the night before anyway. It hadn't helped that her connecting flight from Rome had been delayed for hours too. All she could think of was falling into her bed at the hotel.

The thought of getting into her comfy pajamas after taking a long, hot bath gave her something to look forward to. The seatbelt sign dinged and lit up again and she squeezed herself out of the rest room and made her way back to her seat.

She stared at the handful of business-suited people on the plane. It was a much smaller aircraft than the 747 she had boarded at Denver. She was relieved that it would be a short flight because flying in this little dinky plane gave her an uneasy feeling.

About an hour later, she found herself waiting at Verona airport for her luggage. The other passengers, all six of them, only had carry-on bags and were all dressed as though they were on a business trip.

The absence of any other holidaymakers on the plane made her wonder if now was such a good time to be taking a vacation in Verona.

She looked around tiredly. The airport was small and mostly empty. It was quiet. She had never known airports to be quiet. In her entire life, travelling was a buzzing, busy, energetic activity with a hive of people scurrying everywhere.

It wasn't the case here, not in Verona.

She had been watching the dull gray conveyor belt circling around and around and now, as she blinked her eyes, she saw that it was empty. She double-checked the monitor. Her flight number was no longer showing. She glanced at her watch: it was almost seven o'clock. There was hardly any luggage to get off the plane, but it seemed as though the airline luggage handlers had messed up with the little that they had.

Beyond exhaustion, doubts, like vultures circling fallen animals, whirred around in her head. She pondered the wisdom of her decision to follow through with her honeymoon. Wouldn't it have been better to have gone away for a short break nearer home?

She wandered around, looking for signs that might indicate the whereabouts of an Information Desk.

Hope revived her briefly when she saw the brightly colored sign high up in the air a few blocks down. Feeling salvation to be at hand, Ava quickly made her way in that direction, her gaze focused on the face of the clerk who sat at the desk directly beneath the sign.

Her tunnel vision directed her swiftly toward the information desk but a couple yards from it, she collided head on into the solid chest of a tall, dark-haired man. He'd been looking through some signs that he carried in his hands.

Signs that fell to the floor with a thud and scattered everywhere. He mumbled something that sounded like an apology.

It was then that Ava caught sight of the hotel name on them: Casa Adriana.

The name of her hotel.

Help had indeed come. It seemed the hotel had sent someone to pick her up. She hadn't expected it, but now that he was here, she was more than thankful.

Ava unfolded the itinerary she was carrying in her hands to double check the hotel name, and sure enough, it was the Casa Adriana.

The man she had crashed into had bent down and was gathering together the hotel signs that lay scattered all over the floor. Ava immediately got down on the floor to help.

"I'm so sorry," she cried breathlessly, as her bag slipped from her elbow and she half knelt, half bent her knee, to help him.

He looked at her then, the heat from those dark, glittering eyes burning her cheeks. His eyes were the color of dark chocolate. She smiled, feeling herself melting. "Not a problem." He smiled at her, making it almost impossible for her to ignore those full lips and his chiseled jawline.

Oh dear god, she wasn't going to be able to get back up.

The man stood up first and held out his hand. At first she just stared at it blankly, her senses deserting her completely. When he nodded, and looked at her with those penetrating eyes again she took his hand as though it was a lifeline.

He had her covered, good and strong; his firm hand gripped hers and she flew up, straight into his chest again. Embarrassment covered her face as she rebounded back from his taut body. That brief encounter, her body flush against his, was imprinted on her senses.

"I'm so sorry," she mumbled, handing him back his signs.

"That's the second time you've said that." He watched her with something akin to amusement.

The first thing she noticed was that his ripe lips curled up at the edges, and when he smiled his eyes blazed like dark granite stones. The second thing she noticed was that he was impeccably dressed, in a well-cut dark suit with a white shirt. And the third thing she noticed was that he was drop-dead, breath-stoppingly handsome. It immediately made her want to vanish into thin air.

But as their eyes locked, time stopped. Her heart bounced around like a ping-pong ball underneath her ribs.

She had to break the spell. "I'm staying at the Casa Adriana. Did they send you?"

He dipped his head a little, almost in confusion, it seemed like, and then, "Yes. Yes, they did. Shall we go?"

What was happening to her? She'd lost the ability to speak. *Luggage, tell him about the luggage.*

As synapses reconnected and sparked back to life, Ava managed to string a bunch of words together. "I've ...lost my... luggage."

The man twitched his lips. "Let's see if we can fix that for you," he said easily, as though this was no major problem.

Ava felt her heart beginning to slow down, just a little.

Jetlag did not sit well with her at the best of times but now it was clouding her every thought. Now that this man, who might just as well have walked off the catwalks of Milan and into her path at the airport, stood watching her with a twinkle in his eye.

Her legs felt boneless.

She stared at this smoothly sculpted face and was instantly reminded of Rona's warnings which she dismissed immediately. "I'm sorry you had a bad journey coming here. But we'll sort it out. Don't worry."

In that moment, he made her feel taken care of; something that was alien to her, after everything that had happened. It wasn't just the terrible plane journey with its delays and lost luggage but what this journey signified for her: it was meant to herald a new start.

For no reason at all, she felt irrationally emotional and stood up straight staring up at him. "Thank you." Her defenses crumbled like pastry and struggled to keep her emotions in check.

The very act of his kindness had dismantled her guard.

She smiled at him weakly and watched as he leapt into action, summoning the clerk over from the Information desk. He ordered him to chase up the missing luggage.

Then he turned back to Ava. "Forgive me, I seem to have mislaid my customer sheet. I don't have any details for you. Your name?"

"Ava Ramirez. From Denver." She looked at the signs that he carried.

"Welcome to Verona, Ms. Ramirez. My name is Nico." His gaze quickened her pulses.

"Nice to meet you, Nico." She managed a smile but had to look elsewhere before she made a complete fool of herself.

The clerk over by the information desk was walking towards them.

"We're sorry Mr.—"

"Explain." The driver cut him off short.

"The lady's luggage is still at Rome airport. The flight was delayed and it appears that they didn't get the luggage onto the plane in time. It will arrive on the next flight." He looked at Ava apologetically.

"When would that be?" Ava asked, rubbing her forehead with the palm of her hand. She could feel a headache coming on.

The clerk blushed deeply. "Not until tomorrow morning, Madam. I'm sorry."

Ava's hopes deflated. "As long as that? But I don't have anything on me, no clothes, nothing."

"I'm sorry, Madam, but there is nothing I can do."

She gave him a tired smile. "It will turn up when it turns up, I guess. Thank you for following it up."

The clerk looked relieved and then Nico dismissed him.

Now it was just the two of them and she stared at him blankly. "I didn't think my day could get any worse," she muttered, more to herself than to him. But he raised an eyebrow in response. "Don't worry. I'll see to it that you have everything you need. Come, let's get you to the hotel." He led the way out of the airport and Ava followed him. It was just a short distance to the car that was parked just to the side of the small airport. He held the backseat passenger door open for her.

Charmed by his thoughtfulness, Ava could only smile at him again as she clambered into the car. She should have felt lousy and overtired and the thought of having no clothes to change into would have just about tipped the balance of her sanity, but instead she felt alive and excited, and very much looking forward to the ride with this new stranger.

Along the way, she watched him, from her seat at the back, every now and then sneaking a peak into the rear-view mirror, hoping to catch a glimpse of him when his eyes were on the road.

He had his cellphone docked into a device on the dashboard and he had it on loud. He babbled very quickly in Italian to a woman at the other end. Though Ava could hear both of them talking, she had no idea what they were saying.

She thought she heard her name mentioned a few times, and then she thought she heard the name Beachcroft mentioned too, but it couldn't be, could it?

She reasoned that she was so tired that she was starting to hear things.

# CHAPTER FIVE

They travelled in silence most of the thirty-minute journey to the Casa Adriana, a small, discreet yet elegant five-star luxury hotel set just outside the center of Verona.

Ava checked her cell phone and texted her mom to let her know she had arrived safe and well. She didn't feel like speaking to anyone at this moment.

The mere act of landing in Verona and making her way to the hotel where she would have spent her honeymoon with Connor felt strange.

An image of Connor flashed into her mind and she wasn't sure if what she felt was a touch of sadness or relief. But she knew she felt strange.

She looked up into the rearview mirror and saw that the driver was watching her. Obviously embarrassed that he had been caught, he quickly asked, "Are you all right? You seem a little sad."

Thoughtful and telepathic too. Ava didn't want him to be able to read her too easily. She was struggling to put her armor back on. Remember Rona's words, she reminded herself.

Though god only knew, it was hard enough with this man. Of all the people who could have picked her up, trust her to get the one who looked like a rockstar god.

"Tired, more than anything."

"Try not to worry about your luggage. It will arrive."

"I hope so. I'm looking forward to a nice, long bath and—" She instantly regretted saying those words, because his eyes were riveted to hers as they stared at each other in the mirror. She didn't want him to have an image of her naked in the bath but, strangely and for no reason, the idea secretly thrilled her, too.

"Of course." After a pause that seemed to go on forever, he asked, "What brings you to this beautiful part of the country, Ms. Ramirez?"

Ava had closed her eyes for a second and rested her head against the headrest. His question jerked her back to life. "Business," she answered, not wanting to get into the real reason.

There was silence and she felt that he was waiting for her to elaborate. "More like a working holiday." She turned her face towards the window and stared out.

The driver stayed silent and made no further attempts at small talk, much to her relief.

By the time they arrived at the hotel it was dark outside and the evening had a touch of chill about it. Ava walked past the huge terracotta plant pots on either side of the two quaint glass doors, and across the black-and-white-checked marbled floor of the small hotel lobby. The Casa Adriana was small, decadent and with a very classic look and feel about it.

Ava looked up at the glimmering glass chandelier in the center of the square lobby and fell in love with this charming hotel immediately. To one side was the reception desk and behind it stood a petite-sized female receptionist with a warm and welcoming smile. Ava approached the desk.

"Ms. Ramirez, welcome to Casa Adriana," said the receptionist.

"Thank you. I'm so relieved to have made it here at all." A feeling of peace had descended on her as soon as she'd set foot into this charming place.

The woman smiled at her sympathetically. Ava noted the name on her badge. *Gina.*

"I'm sorry for the journey you had, Madam. I hope we can make it up to you."

"These things happen. It's not your fault."

The receptionist handed Ava the key card, the warm smile never once leaving her lips. "Your key, Madam. You have room number eighteen on the first floor. We took the liberty of ordering you some clothes since your luggage won't be here until tomorrow evening."

Surprised by this, Ava looked over at the driver, and saw that he was talking to another hotel assistant nearby. He must have arranged all of this when he made that call en route.

"Thank you. That's very kind of you. Oh, and thank you for sending the driver." She was amazed and surprised by the speed and efficiency with which everything had been taken care of. Perhaps at the end of her stay she'd leave a glowing testimonial in the hotel guest book, if they had one, or maybe even an online review.

"The driver?" Gina looked confused.

Nico appeared by Gina's side. His presence rattled Ava and took her by surprise. "That's quite all right, Madam." Dark eyes glittered again when he smiled.

Ava forgot to breathe.

"Will you be dining here tonight, Madam?" asked Gina.

Dinner had been the last thing on Ava's mind and the receptionist noted her hesitancy.

"Or perhaps, Madam, you would prefer room service?"

As grateful as she was for the driver's thoughtfulness, Ava found herself a little on edge each time he was near. "I don't know. I'm so tired now. Can I decide later?"

"As you wish, Madam."

She needed to keep her distance, and was surprised that he seemed so attentive to her. She was grateful for all he had done, but she was at risk of too much daydreaming about this man, if she let her mind wander.

She'd come here to heal and forget.

Not to get involved with someone.

Not that someone as devastatingly good-looking as this man would ever be interested in someone like her.

Overcome with tiredness, Ava longed to get to her room. "Thank you."

"We will inform you as soon as your luggage arrives, Madam. Have a good evening." The receptionist smiled at her again.

Ava nodded at them and walked up the stairs to her room. The first thing she noticed as she entered was a stack of plain black boxes piled up high on the table at the center of the room. She slipped off her pumps and padded across the richly carpeted floor, her toes sinking into the thick pile with each footstep. Puzzled and with a racing heart, she eagerly opened the first box. Inside were a pair of pajamas: silk, cream-colored, and very reminiscent of the '50s. The second box contained toiletries, toothpaste, a toothbrush, an organic body wash, face cream and eye cream. The third box had a pair of jeans and a few shirts in white, navy blue, and black. They were so casual and so...*her*. She picked up one of the cotton, fitted, long-sleeved shirts and held it to her. This was exactly the type of shirt *she* would have bought.

She presumed this had all been arranged by the driver, which amazed her even more. The man had only seen her for less than twenty minutes before he had, she guessed, made that call, probably to Gina.

Connor would barely be able to gauge her body size, let alone work out her style, even after all these years.

She put down the shirt and picked up the plain white card that lay by the side. It was bordered by a thin embossed gold line, and on it a hand written note in ink, that simply said:

*With compliments of the Casa Adriana. We hope you enjoy your stay.*

At a loss for words, Ava sunk into the large leather seat behind her. Her impressions of this quaint and beautiful hotel quickly shot up another thousandfold. They had, it seemed, thought of everything.

And the driver. This man called Nico, he had a certain presence about him. How lucky she'd been that they'd sent someone to fetch her.

How nice for her that they'd sent him. The man had clearly outdone himself.

She immediately dialed down to reception.

"Hi, I'm calling from room eighteen."

"Good evening, Ms. Ramirez. How can I help you?" Ava immediately recognized Gina's voice.

"Everything is perfect, thank you. In fact, it's amazing. Really. I just wanted to thank you for the clothes and toiletries. It was very thoughtful of you."

"You're welcome, Ms. Ramirez."

Ava smiled. "Would you please pass on my sincere thanks to the driver?"

"The driver?"

"Yes, the driver."

"Ah. Yes, the driver. Certainly, Madam."

She hung up. The obstacles she had faced getting here were immediately forgotten. Holding the silk top of the pajamas against her skin, she felt the cool softness of the fabric and couldn't wait to slip into them. But first she would have a nice long bath; then perhaps she would order room service and sit in the huge super king-sized bed.

Her holiday in Italy had definitely begun and she intended to make the most of it. She laughed out loud and sank her back further into the chair. She was here now, in Verona, for a glorious seven days before heading off to Venice for four more.

Getting here might have been frustrating, but she suddenly felt optimistic again about her trip.

She suddenly felt optimistic about her life.

# CHAPTER SIX

Nico's gaze fixed on Ava as she walked upstairs, oblivious to the fact that he was watching her.

There it was again. His heart was beating faster than usual and it bothered him. It bothered his sensibility that a woman, any woman, could captivate *his* attention the way that Ava just had. He snorted to himself, a half-grunt that quickly changed to a cough when he turned around to see Gina looking at him curiously.

He walked toward her, just as the Fonterellis approached from the opposite direction. The tall and elegant Maria Fonterelli, with her slender arms linked in her husband's, walked past, making sure to catch Nico's eye.

She gave him a lingering gaze and Mr. Fonterelli nodded to him as their paths crossed under the glass chandelier.

"Good evening, sir, Madam," Nico said graciously, waiting for them to pass.

He strode over to Gina. "Thank you for organizing Ms. Ramirez's shopping so quickly, Gina. Good choice."

"You were very exact and correct with your sizing and style, Mr. Cazale," Gina replied slowly.

"Of course." Nico didn't know what else to say. He knew women. He knew their tastes, their styles and their choices. He was an expert at guessing a woman's size as well as her age, and he prided himself on the matter.

Though he had to admit, this Ava Ramirez was unlike most other women. She'd found him attractive, he could tell from that glint in her eye when she'd looked at him, but she hadn't flirted with him at all.

This was something new to him. Women automatically rushed toward him, did just about anything to get his attention and keep it.

*Anything.*

Just as Mrs. Fonterelli had done, even though she had been by her husband's side.

He had been used to such attention from women all his life. It had started way back in his teens. But in recent years, he found the attention he attracted becoming increasingly intrusive, as well as predictable.

There was something else that bothered him now that had never bothered him before. He never knew if women were interested in him as a person or whether it was his money they were after.

He had the money. But it didn't help when women thought he was good looking. His mother had always told him he was handsome. But didn't all mothers say that to their sons?

He missed her dearly. Even now, though it had been five years, he still thought of her. His mother had been the only woman who had loved him for being *him*.

Now he trusted no other woman in his life. He was convinced they saw his family name first, along with his money, or to be precise, his father's wealth, and that was what they wanted above all else.

Ava Ramirez had been different; even though their encounter had been brief, it was something he had never experienced before. A woman who didn't try to hold his attention. If anything, she looked as though she wanted to get to the hotel quickly and run to her room. Which was what she'd done, more or less.

The fact that she'd mistaken him for a hotel driver appealed to him. She looked at him and saw an everyday, regular person, stripped of money and name.

She didn't know who he was. And he liked that more.

It wasn't just her looks. Granted, she was beautiful. Stunning and tall, with those beautiful eyes that haunted him even now as he thought about her; eyes so light and gray, yet sometimes blue. She had him mesmerized.

Yet Ava Ramirez not only had no idea who he was, she hadn't been the slightest bit bothered about flirting with him either. And she oozed this sense of vulnerability, this aura about her that made him feel protective towards her. Heck, yes, he'd drive her to her hotel. Anything to help her out.

He had played along. For now he was content to let her think that he was just what she thought him to be. A hotel driver and nothing more.

"Remember, Gina. I'm just a driver for now. Nico. Okay?"

"A driver..." Gina looked at him in amusement.

"Don't you go saying anything," he warned, with a soft smile on his lips. He'd never be able to pull anything over Gina. She was only a few years' older than him but she had the wisdom of his grandmother.

He shrugged off her inquisitive stare and flicked through the hotel guest book. He'd been at the airport to drop his father off. His father had gone away for a few days on business to look over things at the Cazale Roma, their hotel in Rome.

This meant it would be even easier to pull this off. For the first time ever, Nico was intrigued to find out what it would be like to be around a woman who had no idea about him.

And a woman he found to be very attractive, too.

The fact that the admiration didn't seem to be two ways was something that didn't bother him right now. He'd been avoiding women for a while and kept himself busy at work. His father's watchful eye on him helped keep his thoughts away from his former playboy ways. Nico knew that a lot depended on him. More than that, the Cazale future depended on his progress and results.

But seeing that Ava Ramirez had not behaved as most women usually did towards him, made him curious.

"Mr. Cazale. There's something you need to know." Gina's voice was hushed as she leaned closer to him.

He raised an eyebrow.

"Ava Ramirez is meant to be on her honeymoon."

He flinched and turned his head sharply. "Honeymoon? Are you sure?"

"Of course I'm sure. Didn't you see her wedding ring?" Gina sifted through sheets of paper in her hands.

"On her honeymoon," Nico murmured to himself, before cupping his chin and resting his other arm across his chest. "Where is her husband?"

"I believe he died. I think she's been recently widowed." Gina's voice was somber. "I even called the travel agency to confirm, and they said there had been a terrible incident and that Ava Ramirez had cancelled her husband's seat and would be travelling alone."

"Widowed?" asked Nico in disbelief. He rested both his

hands on the table as if to support himself in light of this shocking news.

But, for some reason, he wasn't completely convinced that this was the truth, despite Gina's amateur sleuthing. He had sensed her melancholy mood on the drive here but even though she seemed tired and down, hers did not appear to be the heartbreaking devastation of a recently widowed woman.

"No wonder she looked so tired and sad. She said it had been a terrible journey just to get here," said Gina with an air of sadness.

"Poor woman," agreed Nico distractedly. He straightened himself up. But then again, maybe it was true. It might explain why she hadn't flirted with him in any way.

He scratched his jaw. This woman was making a heartbreaking trip on what should have been one of the happiest times of her life. He drew a blank. Whatever her story, she was an enigma to him.

And she interested him.

"Gina, let's not jump to any hasty conclusions here. But see to it that Ms. Ramirez still believes that I am the hotel driver."

Without batting a beautifully made up eyelid, Gina responded, "Of course, Mr. Cazale."

"Gina, this also means that you will need to refer to me as Nico for now."

"Of course, Mr. Cazale."

"And that means starting from now," he chided her gently as he flicked through the paperwork. There it was:

*Mr. & Mrs. Connor Beachcroft.*
*Honeymoon suite 7 nights 15th – 21st Feb inclusive.*

He cocked his head, gazing thoughtfully at the booking notes. Something tragic had happened in this woman's life.

Gina nudged him gently. "See?"

Nico made an agreeing noise low in his throat.

"I also took the liberty of removing the complimentary flowers, champagne, and chocolates."

"Good. That was thoughtful of you, Gina."

Gina nodded at him. It seemed as though she wanted to make this poor woman's visit as good as it could be. And Nico could understand why, given the circumstances.

# CHAPTER SEVEN

A va awoke the next morning feeling brighter and happier now that she was on vacation and free to do what she wanted every day. In fact, she felt lighter and happier than she had in weeks.

No work, no commitments, and nothing to worry about. She had not taken on any more copywriting assignments for the past couple of months and had been relying solely on the income from her online children's store.

Her brilliant virtual assistant, Kim, would keep an eye on the site and take care of customer queries and problems as they came up. This was the beauty of running an online store. She could work from anywhere in the world.

Thinking ahead, Ava's goal for this year was to grow her store and offer more products. Soon, she hoped to give up relying on copywriting for work completely and by the end of this year she hoped to make a full-time living from her online store.

She sat alone in a corner of the small yet light and airy dining area where breakfast was being served. It was a conservatory, with big windows overlooking the beautiful gardens of the hotel. A field of green plants and shrubs faced her as she looked out.

It was almost ten o'clock and she hadn't realized that she had slept like a baby. She had been amazed to find that the jeans and white shirt fit her as perfectly as they did. She hoped she remembered to thank the driver for his efforts.

Munching away at her bowl of fruit, Ava flicked through her itinerary. The dining room was all but deserted. A few guests had been leaving as she entered and an elderly couple sat in the far corner.

She glowed with the aura that only a first day on holiday could evoke, a tinge of excitement coloring her every move. As she flicked through her guidebook and glanced at her itinerary, she realized that she had already missed the first of the guided tours, which started at ten in the morning. It was already past ten now. She would never make it to the city center, where the tour started, in time.

Her fork slipped from her fingers and the metal clang of it against the bone china bowl reverberated around the small conservatory. It was quiet here and the elderly couple both looked over at her and smiled before turning back and carrying on with their conversation.

*Damn Connor and his love of guided tours.*

Then it suddenly struck her: Why was she still following the old itinerary?

Before she could answer her own question, Nico, tall and charismatic, appeared before her.

"Good morning, Ms. Ramirez."

Her eyes glanced over his pristine white shirt and smart dark gray trousers, and once again, her heart started to pitter-patter.

"Good morning, Nico." Ava looked up and pushed her bowl away. She cast her eyes toward him, noting his chiseled features and that his dark brown eyes had flecks of amber in them. She hadn't noticed that yesterday.

"Did you sleep well?" he asked, clasping his hands behind his back and standing up straight, almost like a butler.

"I slept really well. So well in fact that I've missed the guided tour to Casa di Giulietta."

"You want to go *there*?" he asked, in a tone that suggested against it.

"I would have gone there. But we had, I mean, I had a guided tour organized for it. Actually, there were quite a few guided trips organized." She trailed off abruptly, remembering all the trips that Connor had insisted they go on, when all along, she hadn't wanted any guided tours at all. She had always preferred to explore new places by herself.

She felt as if the driver was waiting for a response from her.

"My fian—uh." She was flustered and realized that the word tongue-tied meant exactly that. She couldn't get her words out and, in her panic, in reaching out for her coffee cup, she accidentally knocked it over, sending a splintering sound echoing around the glass windows of the small conservatory.

Visibly horrified at the mess she had made, Ava scrambled to her knees to pick up the broken pieces of the cup as the dark liquid began to seep slowly along the floor. It seemed that whenever Nico was around her, she always ended up on her knees, clearing up some mess.

"Please, Ms. Ramirez. It's all right." He held her gently by her elbow and helped her to her feet. The elderly couple had turned to watch the commotion that was taking place.

"I'm so sorry," said Ava in a small voice. She felt the redness creeping into her face. Nico still held her elbow and then, realizing it was no longer necessary, he let it go.

They stood facing each other. Ava's gray-blue eyes

scanned his face and then she looked away. Looking into his eyes was dangerous. And a woman in her shoes should not be attempting to do dangerous things.

"Please," he said softly, "It's really no big deal."

She looked up into Nico's almost jet-black-colored eyes and her insides swirled the way they did when she dropped down at breakneck speed from the top of a rollercoaster loop.

Another hotel assistant rushed to clear up the mess. With his gaze still on her, Nico said in a voice low and gentle, "I can take you to the Casa di Giulietta, Ms. Ramirez. I have to go into town and I can pick you up when you've finished."

No. Not a good idea. This was meant to be a calm, and relaxing vacation, the type where she had plenty of time for contemplation and drawing up life plans.

Five minutes with this man made her senses ignite. Actually, he could do it in two. She wasn't so sure she wanted to spend time contemplating her life, or Connor.

Having her senses on fire was infinitely more appealing; Nico made her feel alive.

"Ms. Ramirez?" He waited for her answer.

"If that's not going to be too much trouble."

"No trouble at all." He gave her another one of his sexy smiles. "Your luggage has arrived. I took the liberty of getting the porter to deliver it to your room, once I saw you were in here. I hope that's okay with you."

"Yes, thank you." She let out a huge sigh of relief. She needed her own toiletries and belongings.

She reasoned that having someone like Nico around would make it easier for her to move on with her life and put the old one—with Connor—behind her.

"Would you like to go now?" Nico asked, watching her anxiously, his eyes not once leaving her face.

"Yes," she said absentmindedly. "I'm ready to move on."

## CHAPTER EIGHT

"Was the room to your satisfaction?" Nico asked. They had been driving for a short while.

Ava smiled. "Yes, thank you. You went to all that trouble to get me the clothes, too, and I appreciate your assistance." He nodded and watched her from his rear view mirror.

"It says here that Juliet's balcony is very popular with tourists and that you can rub Juliet's left breast if you want a new lover," said Ava, carefully reading through her *Lonely Planet Guide To Italy* and then blushing at what she had just read out aloud.

"So legend has it," answered Nico slowly.

"So incredibly romantic," mused Ava, staring out of the window at the lush green countryside. "How long have you been working at the Casa Adriana?"

"Most of my life. Or at least it seems like that."

Ava watched his face in the mirror, unable to read the expression on his lips. She sat back in the plush leather seats and rested her head against the fat headrest.

"A few years," Nico added.

"It's a wonderful hotel," said Ava, lifting her head up

again. "Everything about it is so carefully and meticulously thought out." She looked down at the white shirt she had on; it was one that Gina had bought, she assumed, and it fit her perfectly. How many other hotels would have gone the extra mile?

"I'm glad to hear it." Nico's eyes sparkled when she looked at his reflection in the mirror.

"Whoever owns that hotel—and I know it's not a chain because Conn—" She stopped and caught the driver staring at her again. "Because I see now that privately run hotels have a very unique and distinctive touch about them that make them special." One of the things about Connor was his insistence on staying at only the best and most lavish of places. He wasn't one for seeking out the more well-known chains of hotels. He preferred exclusive, family run hotels that people found by word of mouth. The Casa Adriana was such a hotel.

Her mind drifted to the thought of being here with Connor, but as soon as she looked out of the window, the thought evaporated instantly.

The cobbled and congested streets near the Casa di Giulietta signaled that their short journey was almost at an end. Nico parked up and they got out. Although it was still relatively cold here at this time of the year, the sun was out and it helped to keep the chill out of the air. It was not very busy at the moment but she could imagine the throngs of people who would cluster here during the summer.

"I can show you around if you like," suggested Nico. "But perhaps you would prefer to explore alone?"

"Yes, I would actually." Ava seemed a bit embarrassed to admit this.

"Of course. Take your time. I will be waiting out here for you."

She beamed a smile at him before making her way down

Via Cappello which led to a small courtyard inside which was Juliet's house, the Casa di Giulietta.

As she ambled along the street, the deliciously welcoming aroma of freshly baked bread and pastries seduced her taste buds. She stopped and bought a freshly baked warm pastry, shaped like a heart, with sprinkles of sugar on top. It melted as soon as she took a bite, the buttery, sugary pastry making her wish she had bought another one, or two, at the very least.

She paused as she walked into the courtyard, looking at the statue of Juliet. No way was she going to rub Juliet's left breast. A new lover was the last thing she needed.

Licking the last crumb of the pastry from her lips, Ava looked up at the infamous balcony. She read some of the scattered messages of love scribbled down with hope on paper and bits of scrap and stuck to the walls under the balcony.

Connor had always told her that she was a hopeless romantic. And she had to grudgingly admit that he was right. After all, her wedding date had been set for Valentines Day and here she was staring up at Juliet's balcony outside the Casa di Giulietta, eating a buttery, sugary heart-shaped pastry.

She laughed in spite of herself. Connor had knocked all vestige of romance out of her with one phone call.

She braced herself and walked inside to examine the house.

But as soon as she got inside, the attendants were moving everyone through and out the other end.

The Casa di Giulietta was closing for the afternoon because a wedding was going to take place in this very building later this evening. Ava strained her neck to see over the crowd. The museum attendants were vacating the building and others were bringing through beautiful bouquets of flowers.

A low gasp escaped Ava, and she put her hands to her mouth to stifle it, at the same time holding back an overwhelming urge to vomit. She felt her chest tighten and struggled to find enough air to fill her lungs. All of a sudden, she felt claustrophobic and needed to get out. She could see spots dancing in front of her eyes and she squeezed her way through the now heavy throng that had started to gather as news of an impending wedding went viral around the streets.

She struggled free from the crowd and found herself out in the courtyard once more. The irony of her sorry situation was not lost upon her, and with a heavy heart, she rubbed away the tears that had rolled down her cheeks.

Here she was, she had run away from the ruins of her own wedding and now found herself in the middle of another one.

She wiped her eyes quickly and she rushed out of the courtyard. Her legs moved faster and faster as if she couldn't get away from Juliet's house quick enough.

She marched on and turned a corner that opened up into the local market, but screeched to a halt at the sight of Nico sitting at one of the tables outside. He was sipping what looked like an espresso. Across the table sat a glamorously made up blonde woman, tall, thin and with eyes only for him.

Ava noted that while the woman seemed to have eyes only for Nico, *he* seemed to be more interested in his espresso.

Ava's heart raced as she realized she couldn't avoid going past them unless she turned around and she didn't want to head back toward Juliet's house again.

Wincing with embarrassment, she rubbed her eyes again, making sure there were no telltale tears. She dipped her head down, pushed her sunglasses forward, forced her shoulders back and darted past the two of them.

She prayed that Nico wouldn't see her fleeing the Casa di Giulietta.

## CHAPTER NINE

S he was so fiercely independent, thought Nico, watching Ava as she strode up Via Cappello. So much heartache to deal with and still so defiant and strong. He admired her tenacity.

Watching her from a distance, he noticed that she drew looks from people as she walked past. Maybe it was her height, or her beauty. The sunglasses perched on her head gave her a slight movie star appeal and she did seem to stand out from the crowd.

He shook his head in resignation. Poor woman. Whatever had happened in her life, he had a sense that it had shaken her. Though he'd only met her yesterday, there were times when she appeared lost in thought and far away. And he knew her smiles never lit up her eyes. Sadness definitely lurked all around her.

Yet he still found it hard to believe that she had lost her husband under tragic circumstances. But then again, except for dying, which fool would walk out on a woman like that?

Perhaps her coming here anyway showed her strength of

character; it might even have been her way of dealing with her situation.

Nico shrugged his shoulders and carried on walking down the cobbled street. Soon he reached the design agency which produced the hotel signs for the Casa Adriana. The same signs that Alphonso had forgotten at the airport a week ago, when he had dropped some hotel guests off. The signs that Nico had picked up when Ava had crashed into him.

He stopped in annoyance. He'd forgotten the signs back at the hotel.

*Now what was he supposed to do?* Nico swore under his breath. This was exactly the reason why he'd decided to keep away from women while he focused on getting to grips with the business.

Not that he was chasing Ava. But if his father ever came to hear of him driving a guest around instead of working, there would be hell to pay.

Now that he was here though, why not grab a coffee instead? He walked on until he found a café. Grabbing a newspaper from a vendor nearby, he sat down at an outside table, ordered an espresso and buried his head in the paper.

It gave him the perfect opportunity to look engrossed so that nobody else would recognize him or bother him. It also made keeping an eye on Ava a relatively inconspicuous task.

Not that he was stalking her—he wasn't—but he would at least know when she came out.

"Nico, darling! Whoever are you hiding from?" Silvia Azzarone, tall and angular, bent down and whispered into his ear, at the same time giving him a light peck on his cheek. She had her five-year-old daughter, Alessa, with her. Uninvited, Silvia sank into the seat opposite him, with her back to the footpath.

"Come, Alessa darling, sit down. Where are your manners?" She pointed to the empty chair next to Nico.

"Silvia," said Nico coldly, still holding onto his paper. He put it down for a brief moment and would have carried on reading, but he caught sight of the little girl who was now sitting beside him.

"Good morning, Mr. Cazale," she said. The hard gaze reserved only for Silvia now softened as Nico looked at the beautiful little girl with bright green eyes and a shy expression on her face.

"Hello, Alessa, and how are you today? How's your bear?" He folded his newspaper and placed it on the table next to his espresso before leaning in and giving the teddy bear a little tug on its paw.

Alessa smiled back, lifting her eyes to Nico's face, before lowering them shyly and moving back into her seat. Nico smiled at her, happy to spend time with the little girl and not wanting to waste any more time with the girl's mother.

"Darling. So cold?" Silvia gave Nico an icy smile that made him wince. He was annoyed that she had imposed herself on him. All he had wanted was to take some quiet time away, and now that his father was out of town, he could take that time. He wanted to wait for Ava and to enjoy a paper and a coffee in the meantime. But now Silvia had swooped down upon him.

"Out shopping again, Silvia?" He stared into his espresso cup before downing the strong shot of coffee in one gulp. Then he called the waiter over and ordered another one.

Silvia placed her snakeskin handbag carefully on her lap and sat back. She was perfectly made up and dressed as if she were going to a fashion show and sitting in the front row.

Nico's eyes narrowed as he watched her. "Did you have

anything you needed to see me for? Because I was hoping to have a pleasant day today without any interruptions."

"I was shopping, darling, and then I saw you from across the square. But tell me, what's going on? I know something is, Nico. You *never* take a day off. Of course, now I find myself wondering what Nico Cazale could possibly be doing sitting outside and sipping espresso? This man who suddenly has no time for even his friends?" Silvia crossed her long legs and slid further back into the chair, as her luminous orange nails tapped lightly on the armrest.

Alessa was too preoccupied in her make believe world with her teddy bear to take any notice of the two adults.

Nico eyed the girl's mother and wondered how he could get rid of her quickly. He was sure Ava would be along soon enough and he didn't want the two to meet.

"Nothing that is any of your business, Silvia." He turned to the waiter and took a second cup of espresso. His jaw was tight and his steely grip on the tiny cup handle betrayed the turbulence beneath his quiet exterior.

"Really?" She tilted her head upwards, then leaned toward him. "Your father has you working very hard at the moment, I hear. This is not the Nico that I knew from many years ago. You were just a playboy when I met you. Properly met you, I mean."

"I don't need to prove anything to anyone, Silvia," he remarked coolly. "I know the facts, as do you." He looked over at Alessa and smiled. She was a beautiful little girl and it was impossible to resist her cute little face.

"We'll see about that. We'll see." Silvia seemed to make a hobby out of provoking him. He knew she so enjoyed doing that.

Refusing to rise to the bait, Nico softened his tone, for Alessa's sake, "I know we go back a long way Silvia. But enough is enough. And soon the facts will speak for themselves."

He knew these words would not sit well with Silvia, but he didn't even hear what she said in reply because he saw Ava rushing down the street with her head down, just as she slipped her sunglasses on. He had already seen her tear-stained face and he knew she had been crying. He looked up to catch her eye, but she was so caught up in her thoughts, that she didn't notice him and slipped away.

Silvia glanced at Nico, then turned to look at what had caught his attention all of a sudden. She saw the back of Ava who had disappeared down the street.

"Business calls, I must go," he announced, getting up and trying not to sound as if he was in a hurry. He knelt down beside the little girl and stroked her teddy bear before lightly stroking the little girl's soft, pudgy cheek. "Be good, Alessa, although I know you always are, aren't you?" The little girl nodded, still shy and still not saying a word.

Nico slipped a few notes on the table and started to rush off before he stopped himself and slowed down. He didn't want Silvia to get suspicious.

The last thing he needed was her interference.

# CHAPTER TEN

Ava continued walking, not knowing where she was going. She knew only that she needed to put as much distance as possible between herself and that wedding.

It seemed she was being reminded of the very thing she wanted to forget.

She walked and walked—unsure of where she was or what time it was—until the ball of anger and hurt inside her heart had melted away.

Would anyone ever love her again? Would *she* ever love anyone again? And how would she ever know if the next time would be any different from the last?

Maybe this was what she had been hiding from ever since New Year's Day. That she was unlovable.

*Connor didn't want me. He didn't think I was worth marrying.*

She had put their increasing distance down to wedding stress, but, now that she had time to think about it properly, the problems had been there long before. The spark of love had long dimmed down. She had hidden behind her pretty wedding favors and table settings in order to ignore looking at the fabric of her own relationship.

She had made a great job of dressing up a floundering relationship by wrapping it up in a beautiful wedding. But the core of it, Connor and her, had stopped being cohesive long before the table arrangements had been agreed on. But she had still loved him, knowing that once the wedding stress was over, things would return to normal. He was so overworked too, putting in twelve-to-fifteen-hour days at the firm. They had more of him than she did.

Ava came to a sudden standstill as she found herself outside a small restaurant where a waiter pulled down the canopy and others rushed around getting the tables ready outside.

She took one look at the pretty pink and white tablecloths gently flapping in the breeze and admired the small lilies in shiny red vases. A trace of mouth-watering hot garlic butter floated towards her and she decided she would have her lunch here.

She chose a table where she was shielded from the sun but where she was still far enough outside to watch people walking past. People watching was a favorite pastime of hers.

She ordered quickly, and while she waited for her tuna nicoise salad and her glass of white wine to arrive, Ava looked at her itinerary again, then ripped it to pieces. She would set her own itinerary from now on for this was, after all, her own holiday and it was about time she did the things she wanted in the way she wanted.

Maybe she would visit the Casa di Giulietta towards the end of her stay here in Verona. Or maybe she wouldn't. It wasn't as if she had to make compromises anymore. She could do as she pleased. She was answerable only to herself. It felt good again to have that power, to do as she pleased.

Her colorful and mouthwatering salad soon arrived and instantly put Ava into a better mood. The pink cotton tablecloth flapped gently in the breeze as she raised her glass of wine to her lips and sipped, savoring the taste of it.

All was good in her world again.

She placed her glass down and was about to tuck into her salad when the tall and imposing figure of Nico appeared in front of her, his face etched with concern.

"Ms. Ramirez—are you all right?" he asked, still standing. His face was flushed and she guessed that he must have followed her the entire way.

Ava lowered her glass onto the table and stared up into his face, drawn to those dark chocolate colored eyes. She noted the frown lines on his forehead.

"Yes, I'm fine. Perfectly fine. Why wouldn't I be?" she replied guardedly.

"I thought you seemed a little sad back there." He shuffled his feet, looking unsure about what to do next.

She hadn't yet asked him to sit down. "Why would I be sad?" She pretended to busy herself with her salad. She had to do something, otherwise she'd just sit there admiring his beautiful face.

"I thought you had been crying."

"Have you been following me?" she asked, putting her fork down again.

"No." He coughed lightly. "Yes." He looked a little uncomfortable at the confession. "I saw you coming out of the Casa di Giulietta and I'm certain you looked upset. I was worried. I followed you. I'm sorry."

"I was hoping you wouldn't see me." Ava lifted her glass of wine and almost downed it in one swallow. "You were making eyes at an elegant blonde woman." She tried to make light of the situation.

"If I didn't know you any better, I would say you sound almost annoyed, Ms. Ramirez."

Ava stopped eating once more and coughed. She nearly choked on an olive and reached for her glass of wine. "You flatter yourself. If I'm annoyed it's because I want to enjoy my lunch in peace and you're not letting me have any ... *peace,* that is." She was trying to be stand-off ish and summoned the waiter in order to ask for another glass of wine.

"Would you mind if I joined you?" asked Nico unexpectedly. His hands were clenched into tight balls by his side.

*Not really,* thought Ava, taking a mouthful of salad.

"Actually, no." He took a step back. "It's wrong of me to impose. I'll wait for you near the car. Enjoy your lunch." But he lingered a second longer than he should have before turning to take his leave.

Realizing that she hadn't replied, Ava slammed down her fork. "Stay, Nico. Maybe some company might do me some good."

After all, he was only acting out of concern for her. Obviously she had not been as successful in walking past him and his lady friend as she had hoped. But if he had caught up with her here at the restaurant, it meant that not only had he left his lady friend but also that he had followed her for just under a mile. He had been worried about her, since he obviously knew that she had been crying.

She didn't have the heart to tell him to go away, even though she knew that spending so much time with him was not such a good thing. Not if she wanted to sort out her life. Being in close proximity to Nico did not help her when it came to sorting out her life, or her thoughts.

When he hesitated, she said it again. "Stay, Nico. You're welcome to join me."

"Are you absolutely sure?" he asked. And when she nodded, he sat down, his jaw relaxed again and his wide shoulders eased down.

As soon as he sat a waitress came rushing over.

"Good afternoon, Mr.—"

"I'll have the same please and a Coke." He cut the eager eyed waitress off immediately. Ava watched him as she carried on eating and wondered if he was always this rude to others.

"Have you had an enjoyable visit so far, Ms. Ramirez?"

"Please don't call me, Ms. Ramirez. We've shared a couple of car journeys and now we're having lunch together. You can call me Ava."

"So, how has your day been so far, Ava?"

"Interesting."

"Did you like Juliet's balcony?"

"It was average," she replied, taking a sip of her wine.

Nico lifted an eyebrow in surprise. "Most interesting."

"What's so interesting about that?"

"Most women love the romance of the whole story behind Juliet's balcony."

"I am not most women."

"I can see that."

"Though I confess I am a hopeless romantic at heart. When I admit to it."

The waitress soon arrived with Nico's food. Ava polished off the last of her salad and then sat back replete and content to watch Nico eating. As she looked around, she noticed that the women who walked past their table often stared at Nico. But he was too busy eating his food to notice.

"They were getting ready for a wedding at the house. At Juliet's house," she said after a long silence.

"I see." Nico stopped eating for a moment and looked at

her. He stared so intently at her that she felt his dark eyes were trying to look into the windows of her soul.

"I didn't really get to see anything, so I left."

*Please, please don't ask me why I was crying.*

He drew in a deep breath and said nothing.

"I'd like to use the rest of the day to unwind. It's been a tough day, what with all of the walking," she explained.

"Of course. I understand completely."

They sat for a few minutes, enjoying the afternoon sun. Ava wondered what she would do later that afternoon. Maybe she would take a short nap. Perhaps go for a walk near the hotel and see what the local area had to offer.

Nico was silent for a while and ate the rest of his salad. When he had finished, he pushed his plate away and the waitress came running to clear it from the table.

"I finished before you and she certainly didn't come running to clear my plate away," commented Ava, noticing— now that it had happened more than a few times—of the effect Nico seemed to have on the people around him, especially women.

"Are you jealous?" he asked cheekily, his eyes daring hers and at the same time his lips breaking out into a playful smile. He had taken his suit jacket off and wore a white shirt underneath which made his olive skin look more tanned.

Ava almost laughed out loud. "Jealous? Who, me?" She surveyed him with interest. "Certainly not."

*I hope you're not flirting with me,* she prayed, taking a sip of wine again because she needed to do something with her hands.

Nico rested his elbow on the table and placed his index finger across his chin. As he leaned in toward her, she suddenly caught sight of his Breitling watch. It was almost two o'clock. He smiled at her again, watching her, as he often seemed to do.

*He is flirting with me.* Ava took another sip of wine then realized her glass was empty.

This made him smile even more. She was vaguely conscious of the outline of his biceps through his shirt. It occurred to her that he probably met a wide range of women in his choice of profession and being charming to hotel guests must be something he excelled at.

"Why do the women around here turn to jelly whenever you're around, Nico?" she asked innocently.

He stared at her face for what seemed like the longest time, then replied, "I don't know." Changing the subject, he quickly asked, "What brings you to Italy, Ava?"

The waitress hovered around them and handed out dessert menus. Ava watched in amusement; Nico's total indifference to the waitress and her complete interest in him made for riveting people-watching entertainment.

"Not for me," he handed the waitress back the menu. Ava did the same. "Ava?" Nico was still waiting for her answer and she had drifted off on other thoughts.

He was extremely nosy and she didn't want to talk about herself. "Business and some rest; as I already told you."

"Yes, you did tell me. A working holiday you said. It's peaceful here and the people are friendly. You'll be able to relax here." His face expressed sympathy and Ava wasn't sure where this conversation was going.

"I'm actually looking to source a few products. I have a business that sells products for children, lots of organic products and toys and things."

"You sell these products yourself?" Nico asked.

"On my website, yes. Pretty things, unique and useful things that you can't always find easily in the big stores. Stuff like feeding bottles and bowls that stick onto portable tables that fasten easily to the back of the driver's seat, so that moms can feed their babies on car journeys. Rucksacks that become car seats, stuff like that. Products that are functional and look good, too. I'm always on the lookout for new products. And I really want to grow my business this year." Her voice trailed off as she started to dream about her vision.

Nico listened and watched as Ava gushed about her store. She came alive when she talked about her business.

"It seems to me that you've put your heart and soul into this store."

"Absolutely," replied Ava, rubbing the palms of her hands together. She *was* passionate about her store, and now that she was talking about it she was unable to sit still.

"I have just the place for you," declared Nico. His voice carried a hint of excitement. He arched his eyebrow and glanced at her with expectation. "I'll take you to Montova."

Ava tried hard to conceal her wariness. She didn't want this smooth charmer taking her anywhere. It was bad enough that he had followed her all morning and then invited himself to her lunch, and now he wanted to take her to this strange sounding place with him. She wanted to be alone, not spend all day with this good-looking man.

She rested her index finger against her mouth, but Nico carried on, unfazed by her lack of enthusiasm. "There are many factories and outlets there that you might like. The products are all authentically Italian, so naturally, with the usual Italian flair for style, you're going to find some wonderful products here. I guarantee it." He looked so pleased with himself that Ava found it difficult to turn him down straightaway.

She could see from the fire in his eyes that he was super excited by this new idea of his. But she had been looking forward to having a day to herself to explore, all alone. After all, this had been the whole purpose of her trip to Italy, to think about her future and to spend time alone.

The excitement in Nico's eyes waned when he saw her muted reaction. "Too much too soon?" he asked dejectedly.

Ava stared at the man before her. His calm posture belied the twinkle in his jet-black eyes.

"Well..." She hesitated, putting her glass down slowly. She was here on vacation and perhaps she *could* look around. If he was taking her to an industrial place, she might as well see if she could get some unique products for her business. Why waste the opportunity? After all, she might find some unique things to sell on her site. She did want to expand her offerings, didn't she?

He looked to be waiting for her to make up her mind, but her answer seemed to knock his composure off kilter.

"Won't your boss get angry at you? I mean, is it all right for you to drive me all over the place? Don't you have work to do or something?"

Come to think of it, why was he so intent on showing her around? That he was giving her so much personal attention didn't seem right. Perhaps Rona was right about Italian men after all. Maybe Nico had an ulterior motive for taking her somewhere for the day?

"I have a meeting late tomorrow morning, so I am going there anyway. I thought it might be good for you to have a look since I'm going that way. You don't think I'm going out of my way especially for you, do you?" He ran his hand through his hair again.

"No, no, of course not," said Ava quickly. How presumptuous of her to think this man was doing all of this just for her. Now it was a case of *her* flattering herself with the notion that this handsome-looking man was going out of his way just for her sake.

Feeling silly for thinking exactly that, she asked, "Is it far? It is easy to get to?" Maybe she could secure exclusive distributor rights if she found the right products. It wouldn't do any harm to go and see, now that she was here anyway. Her heart started to beat faster.

"It's less than an hour away. I can take you there and back easily."

"All right, tomorrow."

"Tomorrow then," he said, looking at his watch. "I admire people who have their own businesses. I know how hard it is to do that."

Ava looked puzzled. "But you're just a hotel driver." She blurted it out before she could stop herself.

"Yes. I am. But I'm hoping one day to run my own hotel. You have to start somewhere."

"And for now, your boss is happy for you to run around and drive me here and there?" she asked playfully. She was starting to enjoy this little banter that they had going.

"Our mission statement is to ensure our guests have the most perfect experience in a home away from home. And I hope, by doing my little bit, that I'm helping you to have a great time here in Verona at least. But at the same time, I did have a business issue to take care of this morning. I'm not just here at your beck and call." He gave her a devilish grin then and her insides turned all fuzzy.

"A hotel driver with a mission statement." She gazed at Nico's chiseled face as if it might hold the answers.

"You see how seriously we take our business here in Italy?" Nico turned around to grab his jacket from the back of the chair and it was then that she saw his Breitling watch. A very expensive watch which she knew probably cost upwards of thousands of dollars. And the reason she knew this was because Connor had always wanted one.

She wondered how well Nico was paid in order to be able to afford one of these. There was obviously much more to him than met the eye.

# CHAPTER ELEVEN

As soon as they arrived back at the Casa Adriana, Nico noticed Ava was busy on her phone. She walked distractedly up the stairs to her room, still flicking buttons rapidly.

On the journey back, she seemed to have a lot of things to handle over there, wherever 'over there' was. Nico had listened in on her conversation and it was obvious that the business was going well and she had a helper, someone called Kim, covering for her. But after the call she seemed sad again.

The visit to the Casa di Giulietta had triggered something. What bad luck for Ava to have witnessed the preparations for a wedding taking place there. It was no wonder that she had been in tears when he had seen her.

The sight of Gina hurrying toward him put a stop to his thoughts.

"Mr. Cazale—Nico—your father called from Rome asking to speak to you."

"Why didn't he just call me on my cell phone?" asked Nico, his frustration mounting quickly.

"Because he obviously expected you to be here at the hotel, taking care of things in his absence."

"I *was* taking care of things." He slowly let out a sigh of annoyance. Gina looked at him curiously.

"I hate lying to him, Mr. Ca—Nico, but I know you're doing your best to prove yourself. And you left the signs behind." She waved the pile of hotel signs at him.

Nico took them from her. "I know. What did you tell him?" He moved to the desk behind reception and flicked through the diary.

"I told him you were out at the back overseeing the supplies delivery." Gina dutifully followed him then winced at his crestfallen expression. She, more than most, understood how hard he tried to prove to his father that he was capable of being the man that his father once was. The problem was that Nico's previous playboy reputation preceded him. Gina also knew that the tragic death of his mother affected him more deeply than he cared to admit.

Nico's father, Mr. Edmondo Cazale, had a bad time dealing with life after the death of his beloved wife, Nico's mother. Gina often told Nico that he wasn't thinking things through properly, especially when it came to the future of the family's successful hotel empire. But she also empathized with him and felt that his father was sometimes too hard on Nico.

"Where's Alphonso?" Nico asked with a hint of irritation in his voice. "My father knows that's not something I would do."

"He's off sick again," Gina answered quietly.

Nico flicked his fingers through the diary, his brow tightening.

"He called to remind you of the three o'clock meeting with the catering suppliers," Gina added.

"It's only a quarter to three now." Nico's brow relaxed. It was purely by luck that he had returned. How could he have forgotten this important meeting? It was something that he had set up himself.

"I'm going to be busy in my office for the next hour, Gina. Do you think you can oversee the supplies delivery in Alphonso's absence?"

"Of course. I'm already on the case."

"Thank you. Sometimes, I don't know what I'd do without you."

"Neither do I," Gina remarked as she casually glanced at some paperwork. He walked over to her and stared at the staff timetable she was perusing. "Is there something else that Alphonso hasn't taken care of?"

"I'm not expecting him in today. And probably not even tomorrow. The rota is done. We're fine."

"You are the main reason we are so efficiently run," said Nico appreciatively.

She smiled at him sweetly. "Your father also asked for you to check the mail in his absence and there are a few phone calls that need your immediate attention. The list is on your father's desk," Gina continued, undeterred by his praises.

"Thank you, Gina." He walked away, lost in thought again as he slipped into the office at the back to prepare for the meeting. He often had problems getting his father to see things from his point of view and no matter how hard Nico tried, he often felt that his father considered him incapable of running the business.

A few years ago that might have been true, but since the death of his mother from cancer five years ago, Nico had learned that life was precious, that his time on this earth was short, and a long life wasn't guaranteed.

Up until the time that his mother had fallen ill, Nico had

never been the type of man to think about the frailty of life. He'd been too busy enjoying it instead, but his mother's death forced him to take a step back and to look at his life and what he had been doing with it.

He no longer wanted to squander his time away.

He wanted to leave a legacy. And he was lucky enough that his father had a legacy to leave him, but his father seemed to waver between leaving the business to him and selling if off. Nico had been focusing his attention on the business, trying to learn the ropes, trying to prove to his father that he could take over the reins.

How he wished his mother had been witness to the type of man he should have become. He loved his father, but it was to his mother that he'd wanted to prove himself and show what he was made of; what he could be, instead of just the fickle romeo the press had painted him as.

But by the time his mother passed away, it was too late, and since her death he had been gripped by a relentless urge to prove himself. He owed it to his beloved mother, and to himself, to make up for his shallow past.

His gaze flickered across the list of people who had called. Many of them would only deal with his father. These men were the big players, owners of large hotel chains, and they had an eye on the Cazale group of hotels.

It was to be expected ever since his father had leaked out suggestions that he might be interested in selling parts of his empire for the right price.

Nico grabbed the letter opener and ripped open the letters that had arrived for his father, sorting them out into degrees of importance and throwing away the junk mail. He skimmed through the rest of the letters but there was nothing that he could reply to immediately. His father had only wanted Nico to let him know of any potentially urgent business matters that required his immediate attention.

He sunk into his father's executive chair and clasped his hands together, resting them on his stomach. He felt useless because he couldn't do much except for tending to the day to day running of the hotel. His father hadn't given him the reins to make any business decisions at a high level. As far as his father was concerned, just because Nico was the only child of Edmondo Cazale, did not automatically give him the keys to the empire.

Nico understood that. He had never expected an easy ticket to everything his father had worked so tirelessly to create. But he wished his father would trust him more.

How could he prove himself fully capable to his father if his father didn't relax his reins a little?

Although the Cazale hotel business was successful, bigger chains were springing up everywhere and his family's brand of upscale boutique hotels were often in competition with the bigger and cheaper alternatives.

Now that the news had come out—that Edmondo Cazale was possibly looking for buyers for the eight hotels owned by the Cazale family up and down the length of Italy—these bigger hotel groups were interested in making a deal.

It was up to Nico to convince his father not to sell, and to instead let him take charge and lead the company to bigger and better successes. In over a year he had done many things and while it would take time for the results to filter through, he could see small, positive differences being made.

But he Nico feared that this still might not be enough for his father. His father had become a broken man after the death of his wife and a driving factor to sell the business was further motivated by his wish to live his twilight years in peace.

But things had changed. Nico had changed; he would prove to his father just how capable he was of taking the helm.

He wouldn't do it alone. He wouldn't let his father just give up and leave everything that he had built to someone else to takeover and ruin.

No way.

Nico intended to show his father that it was time to take the Cazale empire to another level.

But first, he had to show his father that he could run the business at all.

# CHAPTER TWELVE

A va lay on the bed on her side with her laptop in front of her and flicked through the emails in her mailbox, quickly responding to them each in turn.

These were items that Kim had forwarded on to her and that required her attention. Thankfully, they were only minor matters. Her helper seemed to be handling everything pretty well by herself.

Unfortunately, the same could not be said of Ava's mother. Elsa Ramirez was worried sick about her daughter and had resorted to emailing her frequently, especially when Ava didn't respond to her phone calls or her messages.

In her latest email Elsa had spent the better part of two pages lamenting over lost loves and telling Ava that Connor had made a bad mistake, a mistake he would regret for the rest of his life, but that she now needed to move on.

"You'll find someone new to love, someone who is worthy of you," was what her mother had written in the last email Ava had received. She typed out her reply:

*"Don't worry, Mom. I'm having the time of my life over*

*here. I've met a tall, dark and devastatingly handsome hotel driver. He is fast helping me to get over Connor."*

She grinned to herself wickedly and almost hit the SEND button, before deleting the last two sentences. Then she shut her laptop and lay on her back, feeling the cool satin comforter against her hands as she spread her arms out on the bed and stared at the painted ceilings adorned with beautiful Frescoes. This hotel and everything about it was uniquely special.

And then of course there was Nico.

Her heart beat a little faster at the thought of his dark, seductive eyes. Was it only yesterday that they had met at the airport? He'd been so gracious to her from the moment she'd set eyes on him; it seemed there wasn't anything he wouldn't do for her.

*He was so different from Connor.*

She found herself looking forward to seeing him tomorrow and visiting this place called Montova that he seemed so keen for her to see.

———

The next morning Ava woke up, got dressed, and sat downstairs having breakfast.

Nico hadn't told her what time they would be leaving for Montova and she was most definitely curious about it now. If *he* felt sure she would find uniquely Italian products here, *she* was more than excited about going there.

She couldn't put her finger on it, but she sensed that he didn't quite believe her reason for being here. For one thing, he kept on asking her why she was here, as if there was another motive for her visiting Verona.

Of course, he had no idea why she was here. Why would he?

She had just finished her morning coffee when Gina walked up to her, looking slightly awkward and embarrassed at interrupting her.

"Excuse me, Ms. Ramirez, but Nico has asked me to tell you that he was summoned away on another urgent task this morning and unfortunately he will not be able to take you to Montova today. He asked me to give you his sincere apologies as he has already left for the day."

"That's a shame," said Ava, as disappointment set in. "I was looking forward to it, but it can wait." She smiled warmly at Gina, who stood patiently by. "In that case, I'll do some more sightseeing. Is there anything you would recommend?" She slipped on her sunglasses and pushed them upwards so that they rested on her head.

"You might like to visit the Giardino Giusti gardens. They are beautiful and so is the Duomo. And of course there is also Juliet's balcony." Ava winced at the last place of interest. Gina backtracked immediately. "Though I highly recommend the gardens and the cathedral. The balcony is a waste of time," Gina said quickly.

"Been there, done that," muttered Ava to herself as she got up, towering over Gina's tiny frame. She smiled cheerfully at the friendly hotel receptionist. "I'll be fine. I'm more than happy to explore on my own for today anyway."

"Have a good day, Madam," Gina said politely before slipping away discreetly.

Ava spent a luxuriously indulgent day by herself, first visiting the beautifully sculpted gardens and the mansion in the morning, before stopping for lunch at a seafood restaurant. In the afternoon she whiled away the hours at the striking twelfth century Duomo.

When she returned to the hotel in the early evening, she was pleasantly surprised to see Nico standing over by the reception desk, looking at something on the computer.

He glanced up, saw her, then smiled, and she detected that he was more than a little surprised to see her. "Good evening." He nodded.

"Good evening." Ava returned the smile and hoped her cheeks wouldn't blush too much, given the heat that was creeping along her skin. She didn't want to make it too obvious—her delight at seeing him.

There was no sign of Gina, but in her place was another woman, much younger, who was cheerfully registering in a new couple.

"Did you have a good day today?" he asked, cordially enough. It struck her that he had such a strong almost powerful presence, as he stood before her in his dark suit and white shirt, that he looked out of place as her driver.

"I did. I visited the gardens and the cathedral. They were both magnificent. And then I had the most wonderful lunch again."

Nico nodded his head appreciatively. Ava recited what she'd been up to and he listened with interest.

"It was a seafood restaurant called Gioberti's."

"Gioberti's?" Nico's face hardened. A twitch in his jaw resurfaced. "I know the owner, Gioberti," he said slowly.

"Oh, yes, Gioberti." Ava rolled her eyes. She had found the man to be overly attentive to her, to the point of being sickeningly so. She thought she saw a flicker of jealousy on Nico's face. "The food was spectacular though," she recounted, her mouth starting to water again as she remembered the gamberoni. Nico lowered his voice and leaned forward, "I'm so sorry about earlier today."

"Today?"

"I'm sorry about this morning," he said quietly, as if he didn't want the hotel clerk to hear.

"There's nothing to be sorry about. Don't worry. Gina told me first thing in the morning. Maybe we could see Montova some other time?" She tried not to sound too eager, though for some reason she found herself looking forward to going out with him for the day.

"Perhaps the day after tomorrow?" Nico suggested.

"After tomorrow?" She tried not to sound too disappointed at having to wait another day. Then, "After tomorrow, of course. That's good. It works for me."

He nodded again, a twinkle in his eyes acknowledging her. She hesitated. "Although, the day after tomorrow I was planning to go to Pisa."

Nico looked horrified. "Pisa?" he cried incredulously, frowning so hard that his forehead broke out into lines. "There's nothing of interest there. One tower at an angle. Don't bother with it. Save yourself the time and effort of going there and it will certainly save you the disappointment that will definitely await you." He seemed so serious that Ava burst out laughing at him. He apparently didn't think he'd said anything remotely funny and eyed her with suspicion. "Why are you laughing?"

She cupped her hand to her mouth and her long, shiny nails glinting under the light. "It's just that you"—she burst out laughing again—"seem to have blown apart a popular tourist attraction with your cynicism."

Nico looked askance, then shrugged his wide shoulders. "That's my opinion of it and I've been to see it. You, however, are free to make up your own mind."

"All right then. I'll give Pisa a miss. Based on your advice."

"Totally up to you," replied Nico. "I will leave it to you to decide whether you go to Pisa or to Montova, though you did say you were on a working holiday."

Ava stopped laughing. "Montova then. Let me see what's so special about this factory village of yours."

He seemed suitably happier at this news. "Enjoy your day tomorrow."

"I will." She fumbled around in her bag for her cell phone which was now ringing loudly. She glanced at it, then frowned. It was the sixth call from her mother today.

"Is everything all right?" Nico wanted to know. Ava nodded before answering her phone and walking away, making her way up the stairs slowly.

*Why did her mother never stop worrying about her?*

"Hi, Mom. What's up? I have, like five missed calls from you."

"You have five missed calls from me and you're wondering what's up?" Ava could hear the concern in her mother's voice, and she was suddenly worried that something was wrong. She clutched the cell to her ear. "Are you all right, Mom?" She walked into her hotel room, slipped off her jacket and lay down on the bed.

"I'm worried about you, Ava! Five calls to you and no answer," her mother cried. "What's a mother supposed to think?"

Ava groaned and let herself breathe again. Of course, everything was fine. Her mother was fine. Her mother was just being her mother. "Mom, I'm fine. I'm having a wonderful time."

"Now that I know you're safe and well, *I'm* having a wonderful time knowing that *you're* having a wonderful time."

She could hear the relief in her mother's voice, and she imagined her sitting down in her favorite reading chair from where she made her calls or read.

"It's so beautiful here, Mom. I wish you could see it."

"A few days in Italy and you sound like a new person. I'm so glad you went. I knew it would be the right thing for you."

"Rona doesn't think so."

"Rona can't see beyond diapers and poop right now, and she's not getting much sleep either. I'm sure she wishes she were out there with you. But she's glad you got away. She returned the ring by the way."

*The ring.* Connor. A shiver ran up Ava's arms. "Was everything all right ... giving the ring back and all?"

"It must have been. Rona didn't say much about it."

Ava's shoulders slumped. She felt lighter now that the last thing had been done. That final connection, from the ring—the only remaining link to Connor—had been severed forever.

Maybe this would give her some closure.

She took a deep breath and watched her stomach rise and fall as she breathed in and out. "I'm real glad that's done, Mom."

"I know, Ava, I know."

"Mom?" She ran her hand over her stomach and wondered if she should mention the handsome driver she had met. Though it was silly because what was there to say?

"Yes?"

She decided against it and settled for, "I miss you." What would her mother make of it anyway? After all, there was nothing going on except a wisp of attraction on her part. She couldn't gauge Nico's interest in her.

She flushed as she remembered him teasing her. *You don't think I'm doing all this for you, do you?* he had said. He was probably doing nothing more than his working duties required of him.

"I miss you, too, honey. Enjoy the rest of your trip. I love you."

"Bye, Mom, love you, too."

She lay on the bed thinking of Nico's dark eyes, as she yawned, stretched out, then curled up again. Her eyes slowly closed, and she imagined what it might feel like to have his arms wrapped around her waist; to be so close to him that she could look right into his eyes and feel his hot breath on her.

# CHAPTER THIRTEEN

It had been an early morning appointment for Nico. But he was relieved that it was over and done with.

He left the steps of the private hospital and rushed to his car, slamming the car door shut behind him. He turned and waved to Alessa as she got into her mother's car. He hadn't wanted the little girl to experience any pain and, luckily for her, it had been a painless experience.

Luckily for *him*, it had been a quick experience and Alessa hadn't asked any awkward questions.

*Unluckily* for him, Silvia had been in a foul mood the whole time and hadn't been the easiest of people to get on with.

At least it was over and done with.

His shoulders relaxed for the first time that whole morning. This was what he had given up his day at Montova with Ava for. His nostrils flared at the thought of it. Soon, it wouldn't matter. He was sure of the outcome.

His thoughts turned to tomorrow and his outlook immediately brightened. The tightness that had made his eyes heavy and fixed that grouchy look on his face soon melted away.

Despite his earlier resolve, he was finding it difficult to stop thinking about this woman who had suddenly crashed into his life. He wondered if she ever spent any time thinking about him. Whether any of those faraway thoughts—for so often it seemed to him as though she were miles away daydreaming—were about him.

It was such a breath of fresh air to finally meet a woman who knew nothing about him at all. But always at the back of his mind was the niggling thought that her visit to Verona was mired by some sort of tragic circumstance and he found himself often wondering just what it was that had caused her to turn up alone at his hotel.

Despite not knowing what had befallen her, he wanted to do his best to make everything perfect for her. The fact that he was looking forward to spending a whole day with her tomorrow made him feel guilty, and a little excited, for having these feelings at all.

He reasoned that it would be better to spend a day being her friend, than wishing things could be any different. It was okay to feel this attraction, and it was the first time in a long time that he had this way about anyone, but he could not take it any further.

Ava didn't look as though she was interested in him, anyway.

By the time his car pulled into the driveway at the Casa Adriana, his mood had changed completely, and he was eager to get on with the meetings he had lined up for the day.

Getting out of the car and walking toward the hotel entrance, he quickly checked his daily schedule on his Blackberry to make sure he hadn't missed anything important today.

As he bounded up the stone steps leading to the double glass doors, Ava was making her way out. She slipped her cell phone into her bag without looking where she was going and went crashing straight into Nico, sending his Blackberry flying out of his hands. It went scuttling across the ground. A small groan escaped her lips and in an instant she was on the ground, reaching out for it. He bent down at the same time, so close to her that he could almost taste the scented body lotion she had used. For the briefest of seconds, the image of a bare backed Ava, slathering body lotion over herself burst into his mind.

"I might have broken it," she groaned apologetically, as she picked up his Blackberry and examined it in her hand.

"Uhhh," was all Nico could manage as he struggled to shake the image away. "Here, let me see." He reached over to take it from her. Her warm fingers grazed the skin of his palms and sent shockwaves straight to his chest. He pretended to look the Blackberry over. "Looks fine to me. Don't worry about it." He managed to display a degree of calmness that he didn't really feel. He stared at her, his heart beating wildly now that he was so close to her. Her eyes had changed color again and were now a lighter shade of blue in the morning sun.

"I'm so sorry, Nico," Ava said, a worried look on her face, "I have a knack for bumping into you all the time."

"It would seem that way." He smiled at her, not caring in the slightest whether his Blackberry was broken or not. He couldn't get the scent of her out of his senses. All he could see was the clear gray-blue of her eyes and his insides melted.

He felt like a hot-blooded clumsy teenager. Which was a crazy thought, because it had been well over a decade since he had left his teen years. Ava was having an odd effect on him and he couldn't find the right words to say to her. It wasn't that he didn't know what to say. It was that he knew what he *couldn't* say.

There was a line he could not cross, as much as he wanted to. He straightened up, but the calm smile on his face belied the tumultuous feelings stirring inside him. He wanted this woman. But she was a mystery, and he had the feeling that she was not his to have. "It's fine, please don't worry about it." He resisted the urge to touch her face and tell her that it was all right. Instead, he gripped the Blackberry tightly, fighting to keep the feelings that she had stirred up under control.

"Are you sure?" Ava stared up at his face, her eyes searching. He wished she would either leave or let him through because he couldn't stand this close to her any longer without doing something he would later regret.

Probably mistaking his silence for anger about the Blackberry, she said, "I'll get you another one if it's damaged." This time she gazed up at him for the longest time.

"It's fine, Ava, really. Please don't worry about it. I really must get going."

"Busy day today?" She seemed eager to strike up a conversation.

Then he remembered he'd told her he would be tied up for the day. "Yes. Unfortunately. Where are you off to?" he asked, trying to lighten his tone.

"Gina told me to try the Roman Theatre and the Arena, but I'm thinking about going to Milan for the day."

"Milan?" he asked in surprise. "That's over an hour away, by train."

"I like trains," retorted Ava defensively.

"Ahhh. You like shopping, too? If you like shopping, you will love Milan. Most of the women do." But he didn't have Ava down for someone who was so interested in shopping.

"I was going to check out Milan ahead of our trip to Montova."

His insides fluttered with curiosity. "If you want to shop for yourself, then by all means go to Milan. But if you're looking for products for your store, you won't get them in Milan. Montova is much better. I don't want to keep putting you off visiting these places. It seems that's all I am doing at the moment." He tried not to stare too intently at her face as she considered his advice.

"Since you've convinced me to go to this place tomorrow, I won't bother going to Milan today. I'll go to the other places that Gina suggested instead." She got out her sunglasses and slipped them onto her face.

"The arena is a good choice, although it is better when they have operas on." He couldn't help but notice the wedding band on her hand. "Have a good day, Ava." He glanced at her one final time before opening the glass door. "Ciao."

They parted ways, and he continued to watch Ava as she skipped off the steps and headed out of the hotel.

He watched her walking away out of sight and the adoring look on his face changed in an instant as he saw Silvia storming toward him with a look of pure hatred. She blasted in through the double doors and headed straight for him. "You forgot your calculator." She threw the small silver device at him.

The good feeling that Ava had just left him with evaporated into the air.

Silvia had slithered into his path. He hadn't even seen or heard her car pull up. "It's only a calculator, Silvia," he said irritably. "Alessa was bored, so I told her to play with it. I don't even need it back." But he was wise enough to know that this wasn't the real reason for Silvia's visit. She would have found another excuse if it wasn't the calculator.

Silvia's face turned into a tight smile. "Don't worry, darling, you know how much I like to see you." She stormed off, back to her car.

As soon as she said that, Nico knew, without a doubt, that she had seen his exchange with Ava.

With a face like thunder, Nico headed straight toward the reception desk only to find Gina hit him with the words he least expected. "Your father has returned."

The day could not have gotten any worse. Nico placed his hand across his forehead and ran his fingers through his thick, black hair. His father was not going to be very happy with him. But he had to face him no matter what.

"Where is he?" he asked wearily.

"In the office." Gina glanced sideways at the small door behind the hotel reception. "You'd better be quick. He has a meeting with the Luxuriant Group at two."

"He wasn't supposed to be back until tomorrow." Nico tensed his fingers.

"The Luxuriant group brought forward their meeting to today. They have an offer that interested your father greatly."

Nico's shoulders rose and fell sharply as his breathing grew deeper. He walked to the door slowly. He didn't like the sound of this. His father had given him two years to prove himself and he was only halfway through. And doing a good job, too. What was all this about?

The Luxuriant Group was one of the larger groups that had their big, corporate eye on the Cazale hotels. For his father to have curtailed his trip to Rome, meant that he was seriously considering their offer.

He walked through the main office and opened another

door at the side, which led to Edmondo Cazale's office. He knocked before walking in anyway.

His father sat behind the large wooden desk and looked at Nico with his puffy, baggy eyes. Eyes that were once almost jet black in color, eyes which Nico now had, but with old age the brown had been ringed with gray. His father was still handsome, and his almost silver hair gave him a distinguished look that commanded immediate respect.

"There you are." His father slowly put down his pen and clasped his hands together.

"Back so soon, Papa?" Nico looked at his father with a mixture of love and frustration. He already knew why his father had rushed back, but he wanted to hear his father say it.

E dmondo Cazale watched his son walk in and braced himself. He pinched the top of his nose with his forefinger and thumb, massaging it gently. He seemed prone to headaches these days.

"Luxuriant made me an offer; one that sounded too good to be true." He eyed his son carefully. "I finished my meetings in Rome, and I returned early this morning. Where have you been all this time?"

"I had a few things to take care of, Papa. If I had known you were coming today, I would have picked you up from the airport myself."

"It doesn't matter. I'm here now." Edmondo clasped his wrinkled hands together once more and nodded toward the empty chair in front of him, beckoning his son to sit down.

Edmondo sensed irritation from his son. "Why are you even considering the Luxuriant offer? My time isn't up yet. I know you don't think I'm capable of running your hotels yet,

Papa, but you're a man of your word. You always have been. Why the sudden interest in Luxuriant?"

"As I told you, son, they have made a good offer."

Nico's eyes flashed with anger. "Good enough for you to go back on your word to me? You told me I had two years to prove myself. I'm only halfway through so far and you admit that I've made good progress."

Edmondo said nothing for a while, then, "I see you're already looking at changing all of our suppliers. Why? These are people that we have used and trusted for so many years."

Nico stared at him with a hardened expression. "Papa, running a hotel business isn't so much about efficiency, figures and profits and losses. It's more about the personal touch and relationships, now more than ever."

"Here we go again." Edmondo had heard this before and couldn't relate to what Nico was talking about. Had the world changed that much in forty years? Surely hotels were still places for people to enjoy themselves away from home?

People still wanted clean and comfortable beds, clean rooms, a nice enough décor, good food and a pleasing garden or other places of beauty nearby. This was what he believed, and it had served him well so far. He should know; he had built up eight thriving hotels in the last forty years, but this last decade had proved difficult. His share of the hotel business had been slowly decreasing; he was getting squeezed out by the bigger chains that offered cheap deals and holiday packages and the Cazale hotels could no longer compete effectively.

His son had enjoyed the trappings of Edmondo's hard-earned riches for so long and now seemed to think that he could turn it all around. Nico believed the hotel business was more than just a commodity. He had this idea that people wanted an experience, over and above the clean beds, nice food, nice rooms and good services. He believed that the personal touch, little things such as giving the customer their own favorite blend of coffee, as opposed to having one type of coffee served throughout the hotel, was something small that the customer remembered, appreciated and came back for again and again.

His son was always telling him that happy customers spread their recommendations by telling friends and family about the wonderful hotels they had stayed at, and, according to Nico, there was no better recommendation than word of mouth. It grew their business better than any expensive advertisement could.

*As if this was something that would give them repeat business.* Edmondo Cazale scoffed at the idea. He wasn't fully convinced, but he was slowly starting to see that what Nico was saying might hold a grain of truth.

It was true that there had been an increase in visitors to the hotel, especially at the Casa Adriana, which was the main hotel and their base. It was here also that Nico tried out his various ideas and theories.

So far, Nico was producing results.

But Edmondo needed more proof over a longer time period, because he didn't really want to sell out. He wanted to keep his hard-earned business in the family, but he also wanted to slow down and take a back seat; enjoy life and doing the little things. He needed to be sure that if he was handing his precious business over to Nico, that the business was going to thrive.

Nico wasn't going to get the Cazale business on a plate. He needed to work for it and prove himself consistently first. And lately Edmondo hadn't felt that his son was being consistent.

There were other things too. Rumors that persisted, and

Edmondo had taken a back seat, patiently waiting for Nico to take charge and fix matters. All these things floated around in Edmondo Cazale's head as he heard his son remonstrate with him about his decision to consider the Luxuriant Group's offer.

"You can't sell out, Papa. You can't." Nico was resolute.

"I'm not selling out, son. I want to retire and spend my twilight years tending to my garden, enjoying a glass of wine and reading a good book. I want to savor watching the sunset. Not a day goes by that I don't think of your mother. But she is gone and I don't have the will to carry on being this busy much longer."

"But I have the will, Papa. I can do this."

"You can? But do you want to?" Edmondo asked softly.

"Yes!" Nico bolted forward, spreading his arms out on the table. "Tell me something, Papa. If you compare the visitor figures to last year, do you not see an increase? Even if very small, is there not an increase, nevertheless?"

Reluctantly, Edmondo Cazale nodded. The visitor uptake had been decreasing for the past seven years, but it had started to slowly pick up again in the last two quarters. It had all been down to Nico.

Edmondo cleared his throat. "There is another option," he said reluctantly; it was something he didn't even want to consider, but he was most curious to hear his son's take on it. "Vicenzo Azzarone is keen on doing a deal that will benefit both of us."

Nico's face darkened. He stood up and paced the room. Any mention of the Azzarone name turned Nico's mood black. "Why would you even consider him? I want no part of anything to do with the Azzarones."

"You used to be good friends with Silvia and she's still so fond of you."

"Yes, Papa, a long time ago."

"Her father sees you as a possible heir to both his and our fortunes."

"Never! Apart from the fact that I have no feelings whatsoever for his daughter, he build his empire the hard way like you did, Papa. His business is built on shifting sands. Any time soon, the puppet masters pulling his strings can change it all. You're nothing like that. It worries me that you think we could combine our businesses together. Don't tarnish the Cazale name needlessly."

Edmondo relaxed a little. Perhaps Nico was growing a head for the business and doing business the proper way, just as he had done, working from the ground up. Unlike the Azzarone empire, most of which had been founded on dishonesty and by building new hotels by knocking down people's homes.

Silvia's father, Vicenzo Azzarone had driven hundreds, if not thousands of families out of their homes decades ago. It was the type of business that Edmondo Cazale wanted to distance himself from.

Edmondo frowned, an unease settling in his stomach.

"Say it, Papa. What is it?" Nico advanced towards him.

"There are rumors. There have always been..." He drifted off, unable to finish the sentence.

"Don't worry about Silvia, Papa," Nico said quietly. He sat back down again.

"It's not Silvia I'm worried about. Alessa is the one caught up in everything."

"I'm taking care of it, Papa. You must trust me."

Edmondo heeded his son's words. It was what his darling wife, Nico's mother, would have wanted him to do. "All right, Nico. All right. I gave you two years. You're halfway through it, and I will honor my end of our deal."

Watching his father carefully, Nico replied, "You know I can do this, Papa. Deep down inside you know I can. You've seen the figures and you know they are changing because of the small things I have done. I'll prove to you that you don't need to sell out. You don't need to see the Luxuriant Group. You don't need anyone." His eyes blazed into his father's.

Edmondo stared back calmly. "Then show me. But I *will* have the meeting with the Luxuriant Group."

Nico bounced out of his seat, his fists clenched as he raised his body to his full height. He crossed his arms. "So be it. You see them and let me carry on with my own plans."

Edmondo nodded in agreement. There was nothing else to say. He watched Nico leave, slamming the door behind him.

He would meet with the Luxuriant Group, if only to keep his options open.

# CHAPTER FOURTEEN

I t was just after breakfast and Ava was ready and waiting for Nico in the hotel dining room. She was trying very hard not to make it look so blatantly obvious that she was looking forward to seeing him again.

As she fidgeted with her bag and then her cell and then her diary, two things came to mind. One was that she was already halfway through her stay in Verona; time had flown so fast that it seemed like only yesterday when she had arrived here sad, frustrated and overtired. The second thing she realized was that despite making plans to visit Milan, Pisa, and Florence, she hadn't visited any of these places.

In fact, she hadn't even left Verona.

"Ready?" asked Nico suddenly appearing in front of her. As he stood before her in a pale gray suit, a white shirt and a dark blue tie with silver embossed squares, she caught her breath and hoped she had made no sound. He looked devastatingly handsome.

And he took her breath away.

She managed to hold eye contact with him for a few seconds before she looked away sharply, not wanting to reveal any of the thoughts that had suddenly taken over her mind. She managed a hint of a smile and immediately pulled her sunglasses down to shield her eyes, even though they were still inside the hotel.

She felt the need to hide her eyes, and most especially her feelings for him, from him.

"Are you ready? I have to see some suppliers for a few things at eleven. Shall we get going?" The keys to his car jangled in his hands.

She followed him out of the dining room and they passed Gina who was busy on the phone. Ava waved to her as they walked past.

Did she work all day and night? Gina was always behind the desk no matter what time it was. There were a few hotel staff, discreet, friendly and unobtrusive, but even for a hotel of this size Ava had mostly only ever seen Gina here.

Nico strode over to the door at the passenger side behind the driver's seat and held it open.

"You don't have to do that." Ava slipped past him and into the cool black interior of the car.

"But we do," replied Nico giving her one of his relaxed smiles before taking off his jacket and getting in at the driver's side. He folded his jacket and placed it down on the seat next to him, not before Ava had seen a glimpse of the Armani label.

"You look different today," she commented.

"Oh?" Nico gazed at her reflection in the mirror. "I assure you there is nothing different about me," he said lightly, as a quiet hush filled the air.

Yet Ava felt there was. He was nice enough to her, but she felt a slight easing off on his part, a subtle distancing. Or was she over imagining these things? Was it that she wanted more from him?

And another thing, she'd had this vague and intangible

feeling from the beginning, but the more time they spent together, the stronger it got. Things just didn't fit. His watch, his suit, his manner, his style, his meetings. None of it fit anymore. The idea that he might be lying to her disturbed her. This was what had been rankling her thoughts lately.

Trust was important, especially after what Connor had done to her.

There was no reason for Nico to lie to her, was there? She didn't care who he was.

"You look more relaxed now that you have spent a few days in our city. You look happier. The air has done you good. Wouldn't you agree?" He smiled at her amicably in the rearview mirror, clearly unaware of the disturbing thoughts going through Ava's mind.

"I completely agree."

"But your stay will be over soon?" he asked.

She thought she detected a touch of wistfulness in his tone, although she might have imagined it. "Soon," she replied, just as sadly.

After a drive that took just under an hour, they were out in the middle of the countryside. It was rural with acres of green all around and then, appearing like a strip of gravel amid the greenery, was the industrial center known as Montova: long rows of factories and warehouses, with smaller shops and retail units here and there.

The grayness of Montova grew larger the closer they got until eventually they drove through the large entrance gates and Nico parked the car.

"This is Montova?" asked Ava, getting out of the car and looking all around her.

"Yes," replied Nico enthusiastically.

"And you expect me to find new products *here*?" she asked dubiously.

Instead of replying, Nico raised his eyebrows and nodded his head. "Come," he said, beckoning her with his hand as she caught sight of the huge watch on his wrist again. It was hard to miss, because it was so ridiculously big.

Her excitement at looking around Montova disappeared again as she looked at his watch. Once again, she eyed him suspiciously.

"Come? Where?" Her tone had lost some of its earlier exuberance.

"To find products that your customers back in America are sure to love. Here in Montova are manufacturers and suppliers that produce some of the finest products. I am sure you will find things here that you can sell in your store, things that nobody sells over there."

"If you insist," said Ava, walking slowly by his side. Something was bothering her, and she couldn't ignore it any longer. "What are you here for, Nico? What meeting could a hotel driver have to make on a trip forty minutes away from his hotel?" She could see that the question bothered him and watched his jaw twitch again. It was a sure sign that something was up. She continued. "Your boss must be a lenient man to allow you the luxury of travelling around all over the place and doing as you please."

Nico's eyes narrowed and his face lost a little of its former exuberance. "Is that what you think I'm doing—whatever I please?"

"Aren't you?" she shot back, then wished she hadn't started this conversation. She was beginning to feel foolish. This man was being kind and doing things that could benefit her and here she was, questioning his every motive.

She tried to reason with herself; she was reacting this way because she found it difficult to trust anyone now, especially men. She didn't know what Nico's motives were and she had to be careful.

She didn't want to get mixed up in something that would only hurt her again.

Ignoring her direct question, Nico replied, "My boss is a good man, for sure." But he didn't elaborate further. "Shall we go?"

She followed him reluctantly, knowing that he was not being honest with her. Yet he seemed too excited and so eager to make this a good day for her that she was torn. Torn between wondering what secrets he was hiding and why, and at the same time unable to hold back the delicious feeling of anticipation welling up inside her at the thought of simply being with him.

Nico seemed to be in a rush and Ava knew he had an eleven o'clock meeting and yet it was still only ten o'clock. They walked along the narrow, cobbled streets. The town was busy, buzzing with people. It was a manufacturing epicenter. Nico pointed out lots of different factories and large stores along the way as they walked.

Ava stared at a large warehouse across the street that caught her eye. It was the lime, purple, and yellow shop front that attracted her attention at first. The simple sign said, *Andrea's Home Supplies and Furnishings.*

"You like that?" he asked, coming to stop by her side and following her gaze. "I know the owner there and I'm sure if you find something you need, we might be able to get you a better deal." She could feel his presence so strongly beside her. They were standing on the pavement, staring at the shop front ahead of them. Yet Ava's mind was a turmoil of emotions.

Everything had turned confusing suddenly. She was starting to find that Nico had this effect on her more as time went by. She felt giddy and self-conscious around him. Knowing her feelings intuitively, she realized that this could only mean one thing: that she was attracted to him.

She was treading in dangerous waters again, but she couldn't afford to risk getting involved even if the temptation was as great as it was now with this handsome man who seemed to only want to make things better for her.

But why?

Why did he want to help her?

She was certain that he was lying to her, and it made her once again dubious and untrusting of him.

"Hey," he said turning to her when she had been quiet for more than a few minutes. His fingers lightly brushed hers. "What's the matter?" His touch startled her out of her reverie, and she moved her hand away, holding onto her bag tightly for fear he might find it again.

She shifted her gaze from the shop front to his handsome face and searched his expression for clues as to what was hidden beneath. "Nothing's the matter," she lied, sliding her free hand into her front jeans pocket.

"You will find a lot of things here for your business. I want you to make the most of this trip, Ava. You did say this was a working holiday for you, and it this can help your business, it's a good thing, no?" He was trying to cheer her up, but she felt more alone and forlorn than ever.

She couldn't explain the feelings stirring inside her and the guilt that was washing over her because she was attracted to this man. "Why do you care so much about my business?" she asked, turning away from him and stepping down onto the cobbled street.

She didn't look behind to see if he was coming, and instead walked slowly toward the warehouse. Two large strides were all it took for Nico to overtake her and to stand before her, blocking her right of way.

This time his face was sad, and he was quieter than his earlier exuberant self. "I don't mean to upset you, but I can see that I have. I'm sorry, even though I don't know what I've done."

Ava groaned. Now he was being too damn nice. It wasn't fair. He was always too damn nice. He took her everywhere, and this man could probably have any woman he wanted. Yet he seemed hell-bent on making sure *he* was at *her* beck and call.

She was nobody to him. So why did he care so much?

"Stop apologizing, Nico. You're always so apologetic and kind and gentle around me. Why?"

He stared back at her and she felt that there was something he wanted to say, as if it was almost on the tip of his tongue, but he stopped himself. "You are a good woman. You are a guest at our hotel. I want you to enjoy your visit. Does it have to mean any more than that?"

She cocked her head. No, there was more to his behavior than this. She'd been to Italy before and nowhere on any of her travels did any hostel or hotel owners ever go out of their way as much as this man had. She looked at him guardedly.

"There *is* something you're hiding from me. I don't know what, but I know there is something." She challenged him, but he shrugged his shoulders, placing his arms by his sides. As much as she wanted to right now, she couldn't look away. Even as they stood face-to-face in the middle of the street, he was drawing looks from women as they walked past.

A woman was heading toward him; she was a petite, thin woman with a lush mane of almost black hair carelessly pulled back into a ponytail. She walked quickly to them and since Nico had his back turned, he didn't see her coming.

"Nico!" she cried happily, when she was almost upon him. No sooner had she spoken his name than Nico turned around and gave her a big hug. "Andrea. We were just talking about you," he said affectionately.

The woman turned toward Ava with a smile and her hand outstretched. "Only good things I hope." She shook Ava's hand.

"Naturally," replied Nico good naturedly, "Are there ever any bad things to say about you?" He turned to Ava, "Ava, this is the owner of the warehouse. This is Andrea."

"Aaaaah," said Ava, slowly as she returned the woman's warm smile.

"Some shopping for you? For the baby?" Andrea asked, innocently enough.

Nico scowled and barely managed a "No," and Ava noted that he seemed almost apologetic in his reply.

Ava took rein of the conversation. "I'm looking for some new products to sell. I have an online store for babies and children and I'm looking for new and different things from Italy. My customers always want the latest and best things for their children and Nico says you have lots of products."

"He's absolutely right. I do. Come with me, I'll show you." Andrea gestured for Ava to follow her.

"Will you be all right?" Nico asked, running his hands through his rich black hair.

Ava glanced over at Andrea and then at Nico. "I'll be fine. Good luck with your meeting." It struck her that he had been so concerned for her and her business, that he wasn't at all worried about his own meeting.

"I hope you will like the things I have," said Andrea excitedly, as they walked the few yards down the street and headed into her shop.

"I really like your shop front, especially the bright colors."

Ava looked around at the vast open showroom. "I already know that I'm going to love your products." She headed toward a corner that had already caught her attention.

It was a display of baby cribs. Her customers loved these and had asked for so many bespoke types of cribs. She had never found ones she thought were good enough.

Until now.

# CHAPTER FIFTEEN

An hour later, Nico walked out of the furnishings factory with the smug look of satisfaction of a man who had successfully negotiated a better deal for himself.

He had ordered thicker and more luxuriant towels and 1500-thread-count Egyptian cotton sheets as well as high quality napkins and tableware for the Casa Adriana. This meeting had been long overdue because he wanted to change all the hotel bed linen, towels, and robes to a more expensive brand.

Ordinarily Alphonso, the hotel manager, could have overseen this meeting, but Nico didn't feel he could trust the man to do anything well lately. And Alphonso was still off sick.

No doubt his father would see this as another one of Nico's newfangled ideas, but Nico believed that although these things were costly, they mattered. These were the types of finer details that customers noticed. Those who paid good money expected the very best.

He had recently read a few online reviews of the Casa Adriana and all the comments had been positive. People only made their views known when they were extremely unhappy or extremely pleased with a service, and luckily for him the Casa Adriana was getting five-star reviews for all the right reasons.

He was onto something, and he was doing the right things with moving the hotel forward. Yet at the same time he was going against his father's business ideals. His father believed in squeezing out more profits by spending as little as possible. Nico believed in getting the very best and going all out on service, catering to the smallest of details. He believed this would draw visitors back again and again. He knew this would work. He just hoped he had enough time to prove it to his father.

He turned his wrist and looked at his watch. It was just after noon; time to head back. As he walked out of the factory and along the street leading to Andrea's warehouse, Nico felt the eager anticipation of seeing Ava again. He watched as she came out of the warehouse, then saw her head back in again; she was talking to Andrea in that animated way of hers. He could only guess she had found something she liked for she was gesticulating wildly, unable to keep her arms and hands from moving.

He leaned against the brick wall of the pet warehouse, watching her from a distance. Deep within, he felt the mild stirrings of a slow burning excitement, knowing he was waiting for her and that she would be over in a little while. He liked the idea of that. Then with a jolt he remembered the morning and how tense she had been.

The more he thought about it, the more he realized that she had seen through his mask. She had started to suspect that he was not a hotel driver.

Being with her, although it had been hard to hold back, he had never overstepped his boundary.

He had kept his distance.

But if she'd seen through him, it would explain why she hadn't let up on the questions. He'd had plenty of his own questions for her, but he wanted her to open up to him because she wanted to, not because of his questioning. And so far, the few times he had broached anything, even about her reason for coming here, her responses always indicated to him to back off.

Should he own up?

He wasn't ready to. He liked that she didn't know who he was ... but now she was starting to suspect who he *wasn't*.

He was also aware that Ava's time in Verona was fast coming to an end and the idea saddened him. Even though he didn't really know her, sometimes he felt so in tune with her, as though he could tap into her sadness and make it better. He liked it when he made things better for her and he sincerely hoped this visit to Andrea's shop would be beneficial to her business.

He hoped he would one day meet someone like her; someone unassuming and interested in him as a person and not his money or background.

There could never be anything between them; the timing wasn't right for him, and from the looks of it, Ava had things to deal with, too.

After this trip he wouldn't see her again. So, what was the point in owning up and coming clear?

No, he preferred to leave things as they were.

He looked up to see her walking toward him. The sunlight shimmered on her dark brown hair, coating it with a veil of deep gold. He waited, poised, searching her face for signs of unease, trying to second-guess her mood, but she was smiling at him as she walked towards him. He moved away from the brick wall and headed toward her, his eyes never once leaving her face.

It was at this moment that Nico decided he would take her to Montagnano, the village where he had lived with his mother and grandmother. All of a sudden, he was possessed by a need to show her this place that was so very dear to him. He had a feeling she would appreciate it.

"Did you see anything you liked?" he asked, trying to put on a more business-like face. He noticed that the color of her eyes was ever changing and now they were the lightest blue.

"I could have bought it all," Ava gushed enthusiastically, brushing her hair out of her face.

Nico nodded, pleased to hear that coming with him to Montova had been worth her time. He could see the effervescence about her; she was in good spirits once more and her somber mood of earlier had vanished.

"Andrea will be pleased."

"I like her. She has some beautiful things that I know my customers would love."

"I could help you secure better prices," he offered. They were standing in the middle of the street, facing each other again.

"Why would you do that?"

"Because I know Andrea, as I told you."

But he knew this was not what she was asking.

It was lunchtime and the bicycle bells rang as the school children rode past. The sun shone stronger than before, and the pace of life here seemed slower.

Nico led the way back toward the street where they had parked the car.

"Shouldn't we get something to eat here?" asked Ava, suddenly conscious of the warm and welcoming smells of olive bread and cheese floating high above the air. It was warmer now, so she took off her jacket as she walked.

Nico looked at Ava, not failing to take in her lithe body with its slender shape so noticeable in the fitted dark blue shirt she wore with her beige Capri pants. He ran his fingers over his tie and loosened it slightly, struggling to regain his composure. Clearing his throat, he said, "I wanted to show you a little village, not too far from here, if you'd like to go, of course." He watched her face carefully for her response. She smiled back at him, and he knew that she was all for this excursion.

"I've loved all the places you've taken me to so far," she said in a husky voice, taking out her sunglasses and looking him straight in the eye before slipping them on.

"You will love this then. It's a small village, run-down by five-star tourist standards, but most definitely a beautiful piece of Italy hidden away in its own little corner."

Looking intrigued and even more excited, this time Ava got into the car, choosing to sit in the front seat instead of the passenger seat. Nico raised an eyebrow and placed the jacket that he had taken off in the back instead.

For some reason, it felt just right to have her sitting next to him instead of in the passenger seat behind.

# CHAPTER SIXTEEN

M ontagnano was far from the center of Verona and easily another twenty miles away from Montova. It was off the beaten track and therefore not overrun with many tourists.

They arrived there about half an hour later.

Ava learned that Italians from Rome, Venice, and Florence sought out this little village for its jewelry crafts and artisan pieces. It had a history of jewelers and clockmakers who were revered for their craftsmanship.

*Nico was right*, thought Ava, as she got out of the car and looked around her. From what she could see it looked like a beautiful little village and had a charming, rustic feel about it.

She followed Nico's lead as he slowly started walking. In front of her was a long row of little shops and restaurants. A couple of jewelers, arts and crafts, and fabric stores lay dotted around interspersed with a bakery and various other food places. This quaint little parade that greeted visitors who came to Montagnano was impressive.

As they walked down the narrow cobbled main street, a

dark and dingy-looking shop caught Ava's attention. She walked up to it, looking all over at the displays in the shop window. It was a jeweler's shop and the sign on the shop front said: *Flamentagostini.*

Behind the large window front lay trays of black and maroon colored velvet boxes showing off beautiful pieces of jewelry. A pair of emerald earrings dazzled in a box next to another that boasted a gold and ruby-encrusted cuff. Rows of boxes, arranged with pieces of jewelry set with different stones, glistened in the window.

One box, almost hidden behind one of the black velvet trays, had Ava transfixed. It was a small deep blood red velvet tray, inside which lay an intricately adorned silver and burnished gold bracelet. It was decorated with a cornucopia of gemstones, pearls, diamonds and stones of different color and material, all complimenting each other beautifully. She held her face against the glass window, straining to see further inside, but she was held back by the boundary of the glass.

"You like that?" asked Nico, following Ava's gaze.

"It's beautiful," she said, dreamily.

Nico moved closer to the window and peered in. "I'm not a jewelry man but I have to agree that is a beautiful piece."

"Are they real stones?" asked Ava, seeing that the shop was closed.

Nico chuckled. "Knowing Flamentagostini, most likely yes. Their jewelry can be quite expensive. A lot of Italians come to this place to buy what they consider to be one off pieces."

"Why is the shop closed? It's still early afternoon." She wasn't ready to peel her eyes away from the bracelet.

"Because it's only February. Many of the Italians who come here visit during the summer months and that's when most of these shops will open. The locals don't buy much from here."

"What a shame," she murmured quietly. She stepped back and saw the reflection of Nico and herself in the window. The dark velvet backdrop for the jewelry boxes clearly reflected both their images. Even Nico smiled at her in the window.

*We look almost like a couple out shopping.*

"Hungry?" asked Nico. Ava nodded quickly, eager to break the spell so that she would not dwell on what could not be.

He beckoned her to follow him along the narrow streets, until they went farther behind the façade of shops. Here were side streets full of shops used by everyday people. There was a bakery, a butcher's shop, and a greengrocer. There were no tourist signs here. No advertisements for Coca Cola or Pizza Hut. No Subway or McDonald's.

She looked around and saw a group of young children playing in the streets and older women walked at a leisurely pace along the pavement, their arms full of bags of food. Nico disappeared into a shop just up ahead. She followed him inside and found him talking full throttle to the middle-aged man behind the counter. From their lively faces, it was clear that they knew each other. They were speaking in Italian; Ava smiled back at the man Nico was talking to. She managed to make out her name in their conversation.

"Would you like a panino? Ermete's are the best in the whole of Italy."

"Then the answer is yes," said Ava.

"Any particular filling?" asked Nico.

"You choose," she suggested and waited patiently while the two men swapped more idle talk.

A couple more people walked into the shop, and they

immediately livened up on seeing Nico. Ava stepped out of the way and watched him from a distance. He was so friendly and well mannered, laughing, talking, and the group of people around him seemed very taken by him.

The shop owner handed Nico two panini and after much thanking and refusal of money, at the end of which Nico won, she walked out of the sandwich shop with a warm panino in her hands.

"Why didn't he want to take your money?" Ava wondered how to best attack this warm bread roll with its moist and brightly colored mélange of vegetables for filling.

"Let's take a walk and I'll tell you," Nico suggested.

She peeked inside her roll which was filled to the brim with a dazzling array of sun-dried tomatoes, mozzarella, grilled peppers, roasted eggplant and spinach. She tried to bite into it without getting into a mess, but after a few seconds of dainty eating, she gave up and followed Nico's lead. He ploughed into his roll with gusto, letting the juices drip down, wiping them as they fell.

"You need to eat it when it's hot," he advised, between mouthfuls.

He led her away from the parade of shops to an opening that led out to a gurgling stream. Small bridges were dotted about at equal lengths apart the entire length of the stream and there were numerous wooden benches overlooking it.

He walked past the first three benches, all of which were empty, and sat down on the fourth one. Ava followed close behind and sat down beside him.

They ate in silence as the stream gurgled and passers-by waved at Nico. He acknowledged them with a slight wave of his hand.

Fully sated, Ava breathed a sigh of pure contentment. She rested her arm lazily on the bench armrest and tilted her head back, closing her eyes. It was so peaceful and quiet here. It was as if they had stepped back from the daily grind of the real world and gone to a place where time had ground almost to a stop.

"You were right. That was the best panino I have ever tasted."

"I thought you might agree." Nico wiped his hands on a napkin and handed a clean one to Ava.

After a moment's quiet, he said, "I grew up here. I lived here with my mother and grandmother until I was eleven."

Ava lifted her head up and turned to look at him in surprise. "You grew up here? No wonder they all know you." It was starting to make sense now—why the sandwich maker would not take his money. And all the people who seemed to know him.

Nico's gaze rested in front of him on the stream.  He paused for the longest time and Ava didn't know whether to push him into more conversation or not. She felt that this place was very special to him, so she sat quietly and watched the stream.

Sitting beside him, she felt more content and at peace than she had in months. She turned her gaze to him and found him looking serious again. His jaw was tight, and he was deep in thought. When he finally looked at her, his eyes were moist and shiny. "My grandfather died before I was even born, and my grandmother was all alone. We stayed with her while my father was away on business. He was away a lot and so we stayed here until I was eleven, when my grandmother passed away. Shortly afterwards my father asked me and my mother to live with him, in Verona, where he at last decided to settle some twenty years ago. I had some of the happiest and most carefree times of my life here in this little village."

She placed her hand on his arm very gently and gave it a

little squeeze. "I understand now why you call this your own little piece of heaven." She watched the stream moving lazily along at its own slow pace.

Just then Nico twisted his body, facing her and pointed behind her shoulder. She looked and there, in the middle of the topmost slat of the bench backrest, was a small gold-colored plaque that bore the inscription:

*Riposa in pace Rosella Augeri 1912 – 1993*

Nico traced his finger over it slowly. "This was her most favorite spot. She would sit here and watch the world go by. I used to sit with her. We could have given her a big fancy mausoleum or a garden, but she was a simple woman and she would have appreciated this more."

"It's beautiful," sighed Ava, honored that he had shared such a personal part of himself and his past with her. There was a line of verse in Italian below. "What does it say?"

"She gave peace and comfort to all those who knew her, and we find comfort in knowing that she at last rests in peace." They were both sitting, still half twisted at the waist, almost facing each other as Nico translated the inscription for her. "I have never brought anyone else to this spot," he said finally, as if making an admission.

He took his finger off the plaque and his glittering dark eyes looked back at Ava. His hand dropped down and Ava placed hers gently on top. At the slight touch of her hand, Nico instinctively moved forward, and Ava leant towards him. Their lips were a few inches apart and Ava felt her heart thumping so wildly inside her shirt, she was almost sure that

Nico could hear it. She was so close to his lips that she could feel his warm breath caressing her face and as she closed her eyes and succumbed to the temptation, his warm and gentle lips brushed hers, igniting the spark of passion that had lain dormant for so long.

Nico's hands moved up to softly caress each side of her face and she fell deeper into his embrace, caught up in the headiness of their long, drawn-out kiss.

But all at once, his hands moved down to her arms and he stopped abruptly, pushing away from her. He turned his body to the front and faced the stream instead. "We're getting late. We should start heading back." He was cold and detached all at once.

Ava sat rigidly, too bewildered to take in anything else that was going on around her.

*What had just happened here?*

The moment had taken her completely by surprise. She hadn't realized until now just how strong her feelings for Nico had become. The magic that had hung in the air vanished as fast as it had appeared, and all at once Nico seemed in a hurry to get back. He jumped up from the bench and started to walk away.

Ava found herself getting up and following him, but her mind was still processing what had just taken place.

He *did* have feelings for her. Didn't he?

Yet, at the same time she wasn't sure anymore. He turned hot and cold in an instant. She was fully aware of *her* feelings, but she was left feeling totally confused about his.

That he was in a rush suddenly bothered her. The possibility that he now saw her as an embarrassment bothered her even more.

She needed to know that she mattered, that he felt what she had just felt.

"What just happened, Nico?" She tried to keep the irritation out of her voice. He was walking away so fast that she half ran to keep up with him.

"I remembered I have a meeting later this afternoon." He sounded impatient, as though he couldn't get away from her fast enough. He glanced at her for the first time since he had pulled away. Her eyes met his briefly before he looked away, but Ava had seen the coldness in them.

"You remembered you had a meeting?" She deliberately inflected her voice. "You're always having meetings. Who are you seeing now?" Bitterness glazed her tone.

"My boss." Nico avoided her gaze.

"And who's your boss?"

"Mr. Cazale, the owner of the hotel," said Nico, before adding, "My father."

The complete silence that followed was broken by Ava's derisive laugh. "And all along I'd been thinking that *you* were the *hotel manager*. Turns out that you're even more important than that." She had been almost right; he wasn't just a hotel driver.

Nico stopped in his tracks and turned toward her with such a ferocious look on his face that she stopped suddenly too, not daring to take a step further.

He'd hurt her by the way he had suddenly turned cold after such a tender moment, and she wanted to hurt him back. From the way he responded, she knew that she had.

He glared at her, then cocked his head slowly. "Why would you think I was the manager?" he growled.

Answering him in a voice that was deceptively more confident than she felt, she answered, "Your Breitling watch, your Armani suit, your ability to come and go and do as you please. Maybe things are different here in Italy, but where I come from, hotel drivers don't walk, talk and dress the way you do. Come to think of it, I'm not sure hotel managers do either. It all makes sense now, you being the *owner's son*."

From where she found the nerve to say exactly what she had been thinking she did not know, especially now, when Nico's face looked like thunder. She wanted to cower before him, but her defiance made her stand even more upright.

Nico's eyes never left her face, and she could feel them burning into her. More than that, she sensed that she had somehow let him down, somehow disappointed him. And when he said the next few words, she knew for sure that she had. "Was that why you kissed me? Because you thought I was the hotel manager?" His voice was so condescending that she wished she could turn and run.

"*I* kissed *you*? It takes two. Don't delude yourself into thinking that *I* made the first move." *The cheek of it. Did he really think she had come onto him?*

"Does that change things, now that you know I'm the owner's son?"

He probably thought she was no more than a gold digger after his money. Now she understood why so many women looked at him and why he attracted attention wherever they went. It was because of who he was; not just because of his looks.

It all made sense now. A man like Nico probably had girlfriends everywhere. Before she could utter another word in her defense, Nico shot her down. "You're just like all the others."

He gave her one final look of disgust, as if she were dirt beneath his feet, and walked off toward the street where he had parked the car.

Visibly knocked back, Ava shrank, feeling smaller than ever. She didn't want to look like the whimpering weak woman running after him, so she purposefully lagged behind him and slowly made her way to the car.

This was what he thought of her then—that she was a scheming, gold digger? He had given her no chance to explain herself.

Regardless of what he thought, it didn't matter to her whether he was the owner's son or a driver—what bothered her more was that he probably had women falling at his feet all the time.

For a moment back there he'd made her feel special. But it had been just a moment. He most likely did this with most of the women he chased. Chased them until the thrill was over.

True, he'd been kind to her and given her his time and attention; and as much as she had fought his attentiveness in the beginning, in the end she'd found herself loving it. Without even realizing it, Ava had started to have feelings for this man. And before they'd even really begun anything, he had taken her heart and crushed it.

*To hell with Verona.* Her time here was almost over and soon she would be heading to Venice.

Total silence engulfed the car on their journey back. When they returned, Ava rushed out of the car and banged the door shut, not saying a single word to Nico. She stormed into the main hotel lobby and saw that it was busy today.

Gina and another assistant were dealing with a small party of guests. She paused with relief to see that Nico had not followed her in. She didn't want to see him.

A tall, thin, blonde woman stepped out of the hotel dining room, with a small child carrying a teddy bear. The woman looked vaguely familiar. She smiled at Ava and Ava smiled back, still not sure who she was.

"Enjoying your stay, I hope?" The woman asked her, as

she approached Ava. "Go and wait for me in the dining room, Alessa," she instructed the little girl by her side.

"Have we met before?" asked Ava, watching the little girl holding her bear by the ear. The woman gazed at Ava curiously then held out her hand.

"I'm Silvia Azzarone. We met a few days ago, in Verona, although we didn't *meet* as such. You pretended not to see us and, well, Nico saw you and he seemed quite worried."

Something about the woman's tone instantly put Ava on guard. Verona, a few days ago—she remembered her now. It was the woman who had been sitting with Nico outside. She remembered the child there that day as well.

The woman looked over her shoulder at the child and then turned back to Ava, and when she did, the smile was gone from her face. "Don't get too close to Nico," she warned. There was the tiniest hint of a threat in her words. The unexpected comment from this almost total stranger had Ava at a loss for words.

"What did you just say?" Ava wasn't sure she heard it right the first time.

"I'm telling you to stay away." Silvia smiled sweetly, but then delivered a blow. "We have a child together. Or did he forget to mention that to you?"

The tinny sound of her high stiletto heels clipped sharply on the marble floor as she headed back into the conservatory, leaving Ava standing under the chandelier with her mouth agape.

She felt as though she had been blindsided by a ten-ton truck.

# CHAPTER SEVENTEEN

Nico watched Ava rush out of the car and slam the door hard behind her without so much as a backward glance. They hadn't spoken a word to one another the whole way back.

He punched the steering wheel with his tightly clenched fist and his shoulders rose and fell in line with his heavy, labored breathing. He couldn't move. He needed to calm himself down first.

He hated the way the day had turned out. She had done what they all did, and really, she was no different from the rest of the women he met. As soon as they found out who he was, they changed toward him.

He braced himself as he got out of the car and walked into the hotel, only to see a worried looking Gina standing behind the reception desk. "Your father is waiting for you in his office," she whispered. There was an urgency in her voice that prepared him for what was to come.

No sooner had Gina warned him than Mr. Cazale opened the main door to the office, behind the reception desk. He stood in the doorway glaring at his son. "You're late. And you're the one who called this meeting." His father's tone was cold and quiet. Nico bristled inwardly, knowing that he could not fly off the handle, not now, when the next thirty minutes could change the course of his life.

He drew a sharp intake of breath and then he saw Silvia glide into view, slipping in from the side. Her face was bright, and she wore her usual fake smile.

"Nico, darling, I've missed you so much." She walked to him with arms outstretched, wearing an air of confidence like a shawl. Placing her hands on either side of his shoulders, she leaned in to kiss him on both cheeks.

Her demeanor didn't surprise Nico. He knew she believed that the results would fall in her favor, and she looked smugly upbeat now that she had him in her claws.

When he saw Ava's gaunt face as she slowly walked out behind Silvia, he knew at once what Silvia's whole charade had been about. Unable to contain the slow buildup of anger, he took Silvia's wrists in both his hands and pulled them down, placing them back by her sides. His body was rigid as he started to take a step toward Ava, but Alessa skipped past happily, dragging her teddy bear by its ear. The little girl smiled shyly when she saw Nico and then ran to her mother's side.

Rooted to the spot, the anger inside Nico was insurmountable. He strained to keep his composure. For a few seconds, everyone's eyes were fixed on him until Ava made the first move and rushed upstairs, her hand tightly clasping the handrail as if for support.

Nico watched her, paralyzed; he had seen the hurt in Ava's eyes, but he could not comfort her just yet.

"I'll look after Alessa," Gina offered.

"Would you like to do some drawing with Gina?" asked Silvia. Alessa nodded enthusiastically.

"If you could give her some pencils and some paper." Silvia kissed the little girl.

"I'm sure I could," said Gina coldly.

The older Mr. Cazale smiled as he stepped forward and out into the main lobby to welcome Silvia and Alessa. He greeted them warmly and kissed the little girl, giving her a tight embrace. He beckoned Silvia to follow him into his office, as Gina made a space for Alessa to do her drawings.

Nico watched Silvia head into his father's office and his dark eyes blazed with a searing fury. Silvia's little show had been for his father's sake, as well as for Ava's, and Nico's mind raced with the thought of what Silvia might have said to Ava. He had an idea it was something bad. He had experienced the extent of Silvia's malice and he knew that Silvia had seen him running after Ava that day outside the Casa di Giulietta. She wasn't one to contain her jealousy.

"Nico." His father's voice boomed. With a heavy sigh, Nico followed them, stopping for a moment to look sideways at Gina. "Wish me luck," he said gloomily.

"Good luck," Gina said after him, before turning her attention to the little girl who was busy drawing happy smiling faces on her sheet of paper.

Nico walked into his father's office and closed the door behind him.

"Alessa is not aware of anything?" asked Mr. Cazale carefully, addressing Silvia.

"No. She thinks it's just another visit to the Casa Adriana before going shopping," replied Silvia.

Nico tried to suppress the sarcastic laugh he felt was coming on. He adored Alessa as much as anyone. What was there not to adore? She was a cute five-year-old, happy and carefree and with all the sense of wonder and amazement of a child. She had none of the malice that made up most of her mother's character.

Alessa had been born out of wedlock. Silvia, the daughter of one of the richest men in Verona, and the youngest of four children, had been rather spoiled by her parents. So, when she announced that she was expecting a child, with no marriage in hand, the news shocked her parents, but they stood by her in this conservative country with tight moral values. A child born out of wedlock to such a well-known and respected family was not the norm here.

But Silvia, being stubborn and wanting things her way, had demanded to keep the child. This action of hers was probably the first unselfish and responsible thing she had ever done. The problem arose when she insisted that Nico was the father, pinning all her hopes and dreams on the short summer romance that she and Nico had shared.

For Nico, Silvia had been a comfortable presence, someone he had known since childhood. The news of his mother's illness, just then diagnosed, had been hard to bear. And Silvia, whom his mother had adored, had become close to Nico and had helped him to deal with the soul-destroying news that his mother was terminal.

A few of those comforting nights had led to other things. Shortly afterwards, Silvia announced that she was pregnant with his child. Throughout the years, Nico had strenuously denied this accusation. He chose to ignore it because he knew the depths of Silvia's deceit and knew that she would use anything to possess him.

She claimed that she had loved Nico since they were teenagers, but he didn't feel the same way about her. It wasn't that she was after his money, for she was rich enough in her own right, but she wanted what most other eligible young women in Verona wanted: Nico.

For years Silvia had insisted that Alessa was his, and for years Nico had ignored her. But now that Alessa had turned five, she was starting to ask where her father was.

And although Nico's own father had never pressed for a definite resolution of the matter, Nico knew his father believed the rumors, for he had no reason not to.

The time had now come that Nico had had enough, and he wanted to prove he was not Alessa's father. He didn't want Alessa to start believing her mother's rumors. The child was starting to warm toward him, genuinely believing that he was her father, and he couldn't lie to her. It was more for Alessa than anything else that Nico felt the time was right to resolve this matter for once and for all.

"Are you sure your parents did not want to know about this, Silvia?" asked Mr. Cazale carefully.

Although his father had never actually said it to him, Nico had a feeling that if the results of the blood test showed that Nico was the father, his father would welcome that news anyway. His father had told him often enough of his wish to play with his grandchildren. So, if Alessa was his grandchild at least she was here.

Nico was aware that his father was getting on in years and that he had become a changed man after seeing his wife go so quickly before his eyes. Since then his father had often said that life was fleeting and he didn't know whether he would wake up to see another day.

Once again, Edmondo slowly asked Silvia, "This is a big decision here Silvia. I can get my driver to fetch your parents. There is no need to rush."

"Papa, just get the thing over and done with, please." Nico paced the room, his hands clenched so tightly that the bony knuckles protruded clearly.

In contrast, Silvia lounged on the warm leather sofa, with

one leg crossed over the other and an arm resting lazily on the armrest.

"Are you ready, darling?" She watched Nico with cool calculating eyes. "You should relax. There's no need to worry about anything."

"We'll see," replied Nico savagely. He had been so sure that he wasn't the father, so sure that in the five years past he had never put any more thought into Silvia's constant whines and accusations. He had been glad that his mother hadn't heard any of these. If there was one saving grace about Silvia it was that she had never caused any undue stress to his ill mother.

"You seem so sure, Nico. We'll find out now won't we, darling?" Silvia challenged him, daring him to meet her eyes, but he kept his gaze firmly on the floor.

The test had been carried out a few days ago at the private clinic when Nico had met Silvia and Alessa early in the morning. With them both being from such prominent families it was something that both families wanted kept out of the public eye.

Now that the moment was finally here to declare the outcome, Nico felt unsure for the first time ever. Beads of sweat clung to his forehead. He undid the buttons of his shirt and loosened his tie. Then he took off his jacket and he could feel Silvia's hungry, ice-blue eyes on him. He glanced at her, knowing she was staring at him, at his muscular body, and thinking that any minute now, she would have some sort of legal claim over him.

The large grandfather clock in his father's office struck four and the three of them waited patiently.

This was agony for Nico. He stood with his arms folded across his chest. The sudden knock at the door broke the painful monotony of silence in the room.

It was the family doctor, the only man that Mr. Cazale trusted enough to deal with such a delicate matter. Like Mr. Cazale, the doctor was an elderly man and the two of them had known each other since college.

"We have the results," he said, in a firm voice and handed the letter over to Nico.

"No, please, you go ahead and tell us." Nico pushed the letter back into the doctor's hands.

Everyone stared at the doctor's face in order to glean a clue as to the outcome. Silvia slowly sat upright in the armchair, then leaned forward, placing her elbows on her knees. Nico had uncrossed his arms and took a step towards the doctor. Only the older Mr. Cazale stayed calm and sat just as he had in his armchair.

Knowing that everyone's eyes were on him, the doctor started, in a faltering voice.

"The results of the test prove without a shadow of a doubt"—he looked over at Nico firmly—"that Nico Cazale is *not* the father of Alessa Azzarone."

He handed the letter over to Nico who sprang forward with joy, struggling to contain the enormous surge of relief he felt rising up in his chest. He took the letter gratefully and read it once, then read it a second time before walking over to Silvia victoriously.

"Here you go, Silvia. All the proof you need." He handed her the letter but she had relaxed back on the sofa, her legs still crossed with her arm resting back on the armrest. Nico could tell from the tight frown on her face that she was not at all happy, but the elation in his own heart exploded and drowned out the heaviness he'd felt since he'd walked in.

The doctor took his leave, and soon it was just the three of them left in the study.

Seeing that Silvia refused to take the letter, Nico handed it to his father.

"Don't you want to know who the father is then?" she asked, not caring that Edmondo Cazale was sitting across from her reading the letter.

The old man took off his glasses and gave her a sympathetic look.

"You knew it wasn't Nico, Silvia?" he asked with mild surprise.

But Silvia ignored him. Her eyes hooked on Nico and when he still didn't reply, she asked again, this time her tone more menacing. "Don't you want to know, Nico?" she repeated.

Nico turned around to face her. "No, I couldn't care less. I only care that you look after Alessa. She is a beautiful, innocent little girl who deserves to be loved. I do love her; whether she is my child or not. It's her that I care for and love, Silvia, not you."

With five years of constantly being told that he was the father, there had been moments when Nico had stopped to wonder if perhaps there might have been a mistake. Five years of not knowing had made him sometimes wonder if the endearing little girl was his. And five years of wondering had given him and Alessa a little bond, as tiny as it was, that had blossomed into a fulsome love for the child, as if she were his.

Silvia got up stiffly and grabbed her bag. "Goodbye, Mr. Cazale."

She swept out of the room, leaving a peaceful silence behind her.

# CHAPTER EIGHTEEN

E dmondo sank back into his chair and gazed ahead.
"Are you disappointed, Papa?" Nico asked
tenderly. His father took off his reading glasses and Nico saw
only tiredness and sadness in his eyes. He wasn't sure of how
his father had taken the news.

"I have lived to see many things, Nico," his father
answered wearily, "but up until now, I didn't think I would
see such a display of cold cunning as I have seen with Silvia. I
was disappointed. But frankly, seeing that she already knew,
I'm relieved."

"Relieved?"

"Relieved for you, son. The last thing I would have
wanted is for you to be stuck with a woman such as her."

"You finally found out what I've known for many years?"
asked Nico. It was a huge relief to know that at long last, his
father was on his side, as far as Silvia was concerned.

"I've had the love of a good woman, a great woman for
more than fifty years of my life. I've been lucky—more than
that, I've been blessed. I want the same for you, as any parent
would. All parents want the best for their children. I am

aware that you and your mother paid a price waiting for me in Montagnano, but I wanted to provide a great life for you both. I had to work hard to get that."

Nico pressed his fingers against the edges of his eyelids. They were heavy but his heart was light. The immense feeling of relief overwhelmed him and now his father was sitting with him, and they were talking, not as men fighting to prove themselves, but as equals.  Although he didn't say it in as many words, Nico could see that his father was no longer angry with him.

"I'm sorry that I put you through this, Papa."

"No, I'm sorry I put you through the test. It was a part of my deal, although I never told you."

"What are you talking about, Papa?" Nico asked, feeling nervous.

"When I gave you two years to prove yourself, I wanted to know if you had a passion for the business as I do. But I also wanted you to take responsibility and to own up to your responsibilities no matter what. I can see that you have been working hard trying to pull things together with the hotel, always testing new things. I know the time pressure was resting heavily on you."

"That's fine, Papa, but what has that got to do with the paternity test?" Nico was more confused than ever.

"I wanted to see if you had a passion for the hotel business and whether you had changed from the careless young man you used to be. But, as important as your business knowledge and ambition were to me, I also wanted to see that you were responsible and willing to own up to your responsibilities no matter how heavy they were. I know we never discussed it much, but, as I told you before, there had always been these rumors, about who Alessa's father was. By taking the blood test, which could have gone either way, you showed me that you were ready to accept the responsibility. And that, Nico, is what I have been waiting to see."

"Why didn't you just ask me to take it?"

"Because I can't ask you to become responsible. I needed to see that it was something you were ready for. And you have shown me now that you are. Your reputation before, when your mother was alive, was that of a playboy. I couldn't hand over my hotel empire to a playboy."

"I stopped being a playboy years ago, Papa. Mama's death made me grow up." Nico's voice turned quiet. "I've always known Alessa wasn't mine. Always. Though I admit, for a few minutes there I was worried, life has a way of throwing curve balls at you when you least expect it."

"Why so sure, son?" asked the old man curiously, sliding his glasses back onto his face.

"I was always careful. You always told me to be careful. Silvia knew I took precautions. Over the years she forgot that and became so desperate that she willed herself to believe that the child could be mine somehow."

His father shook his head. "She is desperate. That much I can see now, all too clearly." He folded the letter and handed it over to Nico. "But tell me, Nico, why go through the farce of agreeing to the blood test at all, if you knew for sure?"

Nico looked at his father with a steadfast gaze. "Would you have believed me otherwise?" Silence hung in the air like a cobweb. Only the sound of the grandfather clock striking five broke the spell.

"I've been very harsh on you, son, and I'm sorry. But I can see now that you've changed. You had started to change once your mother passed away. Sometimes it takes these hard lessons in life to make us stop and accept our responsibilities."

Not wanting to let his father take the burden of the guilt Nico added, "It wasn't just that, Papa. I wanted Silvia to know for once and for all. I don't want to have those rumors hanging around my head, following me with my every move. Her father was very anxious for us to get together."

"The Azzarones are a rich family, but their wealth is inherited from many generations of their family. Silvia's father didn't work hard, not like I did. He didn't have to suffer the hardship, the regret of sending his wife and only child away while he built up his business."

Nico nodded in agreement. His father had indeed worked very hard during the early years. And only now, now that Edmondo was telling him, did it occur to Nico that his father had loved and missed him very much while he was growing up, living in the village with his grandmother and mother.

Now, finally, Nico understood the old man's relentless need for Nico to prove himself. Now, he finally saw why his father kept meeting with prospective buyers; because he wanted to see what Nico could do. He'd had to prove himself and part of that had meant showing that he had the guts to take on responsibility—with Alessa—had it come to that.

"You have turned out to be the son and the man your mother and I hoped you would be. You've shown me that you have compassion, empathy, and responsibility. You've always known that Alessa wasn't yours and yet you always treated that child with love and understanding whenever you saw her. I see now that you tolerated her mother when it must have been so hard for you, knowing that she was making all these accusations and everyone else must have thought you were nothing but a spoiled rich son of a hotel owner."

Nico listened quietly, his heart ballooning with happiness.

"So," his father said, in a sterner voice, "I told the Luxuriant group that I had considered their offer in line with the offers from all the other interested parties and that I was no longer interested."

Nico's eyes widened and he sat up to attention. He felt a surge of excitement beginning to flow through his veins.

"I feel you're getting a good grasp for the business. You're taking it to the next level; more luxury and moving upmarket. I never did understand why the bed linen had to be a thousand thread count or above, or why it had to be Egyptian cotton when our own Italian cotton is good enough, but the new guest book and online review system seem to show me otherwise. Gina tells me that people have been commenting on the smallest of things and these are the details that they remember."

"You approve?" Nico couldn't believe his ears.

His father cleared his throat. "The results indicate that you are doing the right things." Nico smiled at his father's inability to give a simple and clear "Yes, but let's take it slowly. I suppose this means that I need to inform those parties who are showing a keen interest that our empire is no longer for the taking. The Cazales are more than capable of running this business successfully."

"And maybe expanding out, slowly?" Nico suggested. His father nodded in agreement. "It won't be easy, son. The business has become harder in recent years. Perhaps what is needed is new blood. *You.*"

"We'll create the best hotel experience for our guests," Nico said carefully. "They will love their stay so much they will come back again and again and tell all their friends and families."

His father put his fingers together and rested his chin on them. "I like the sound of that very much."

The two men sat with a mutual understanding dawning

between them. Nico sensed they'd reached a new phase in their relationship.

"One last thing, son. No pressure but, maybe, before I grow exceptionally old and unable to see, do you think you might settle down someday? I quite like the idea of gardening with my grandchildren." The old man smiled, a warm, comfortable smile.

Nico got up and shook his father's hand. Then he clasped him tightly by the arm and hugged him. "One thing at a time, Papa," he replied, a small smile playing on lips.

He came came out of his father's office to find Gina waiting for him. Silvia and Alessa were nowhere to be seen, and while Gina looked worried, Nico's thoughts were on Ava. "What's wrong?"

"We've had a problem with the electrics in the kitchen. The chef complained of it over a week ago and I thought Alphonso was looking at it."

Predicting the obvious, Nico frowned. "But he didn't?"

Gina shook her head. "And now there is no hot water or electricity in the kitchen. Which means we are not going to be able to get dinner ready for this evening unless we get it fixed immediately."

Nico tried to contain his anger. Lately Alphonso, the old hotel manager, had started to forget a lot of things. For a man supposedly in charge, he wasn't good at leading by example, and he often forgot the smallest of things, which then escalated to bigger problems, as was the case so clearly now. "He's been off sick, hasn't he?"

"He was, but he came back today."

"Then where is he?" Nico growled, his irritation growing by the minute. This would not do. He would need to look into getting a replacement for Alphonso.

"He went home around two o'clock saying he didn't think he had fully recovered. Shall I call him?"

Nico inhaled sharply. "No." He flicked through the sheaf of papers that Gina had passed him. "Let's leave Alphonso out of the picture. He's done enough damage for now," he muttered, quickly scanning through the paperwork that contained the invoices from when the kitchen had first been installed. He reached for the phone, having found the number of the man who had done the first installation.

Gina stopped him. "That business has folded," she informed him, moving his hand away. "I called and they no longer appear to be in business. The place is now a pizzeria, believe it or not. I took the liberty of getting a few quotes from some of the electricians around here. Three of them are arriving here within the next hour to give me a free quote."

Nico stood back, one arm across his chest with the elbow of the other one resting on it. He cupped his chin with his hand. "You don't need my help, Gina. You've taken care of matters yourself. I'll leave things in your capable hands."

"I'll take care of it," Gina replied, happily.

He didn't need to look too far at all for Alphonso's new replacement. This woman could multitask and handle everything. His fury about Alphonso was starting to abate.

"Let's see what the electricians say, and let's hope they give us reasonable quotes." He moved away, deciding to take another look in the kitchen.

"One more thing," Gina said, but he'd caught sight of another staff member he urgently needed to speak to.

## CHAPTER NINETEEN

At around eleven o'clock the next day, Ava boarded a train from Verona Porta Nuova and by one o'clock she was sitting at an outside table in the Piazza San Marco in Venice, a few days earlier than planned.

Thank goodness the honeymoon had all been paid for in advance otherwise there was no way she would be able to afford the opulent Hotel Sant' Adelina where she had checked into, overlooking the Grand Canal.

She had been lucky that it was still not the peak holiday season here and the hotel manager had been extremely accommodating about letting her have the room a few days early. Though this now meant she had a longer stay here in Venice and would have to pay for the extra days out of her own pocket.

Having a few extra days to spend in Venice was a blessing as far as she was concerned. Verona had been wonderful, that is, until yesterday when her world had fallen apart. Not only had Nico almost accused her of being a gold digger, but he had also brushed her off cruelly and it hurt.

Her heart and mind had craved peace and tranquility, but she had found neither in Verona. All because of him.

At first, Nico had treated her with a tenderness that had slowly crumbled away her defenses. With him she had allowed herself to feel again. And just when she had felt that first glint of raw emotion, and desire flow into her heart, he had discarded her just as quickly.

Then to have Silvia tell her about the child she and Nico had together, had been the final straw.

The man had deceived her so completely.

How could she have been so blind? So stupid?

How could she have let him in?

She was worse off now than she had been when she'd left Denver because now, she was starting to have feelings for this man she hardly knew. She'd almost forgotten about Connor, but now she was going to have to forget about Nico, too.

She stirred her cappuccino for over a minute before realizing that she was going through the motions. Immediately, she stopped, recollecting the events that had ruined what had started to become a wonderful vacation. She had been so busy visiting the sights in Verona and going to different places with Nico that she hadn't done any sightseeing outside of Verona. She had been happy to stay where she was, with Nico.

Her heart missed a beat when she thought of him. It was as though a bullet had grazed her when Silvia had announced that she and Nico had a child together.

Why had he never mentioned anything to her? Maybe he was just a suave, handsome, charmer, nothing more than a playboy who had lured her into thinking he was something else?

And she had fallen for it.

Yet Silvia had wanted Ava to think that she and Nico

were more than friends, though Ava suspected this wasn't somehow true. Who knew? It wouldn't be the first time Ava had been wrong when it came to men.

Or unlucky.

Maybe she had it all wrong?

She thought about the moment yesterday when, recovering from the news of Nico having a child, she saw Nico, Silvia, and the man she assumed to be Nico's father in the hotel lobby.

The sight of the three of them together had firmly put her in her place. They had something together. A bond.

She was just an outsider.

If only she had listened to Rona and never ventured out here.

*How could she end up starting to fall for yet another man who was so wrong for her?*

She sipped her coffee and played around with her panino. This one was double the price and not even one tenth as good as the one she had eaten in Montagnano.

Nico. The bench, the stream, the lunch. Their kiss. Memories of the day flooded back crystal clear. The chatter of people walking around provided welcome background noise to her inner turmoil.

A blip on her phone told her she had a message. She checked and saw it was from her mother. Her mother had stopped mentioning Connor now and her texts were often cautionary in nature: *Enjoy your holiday and don't eat too much seafood. You know how ill it can make you.*

Ava closed the message and stared vacantly out at the square. Her mother never forgot the one-time Ava had reacted to eating fish, in her teen years, and she still saw fit to warn Ava about it. Even though Ava had been happily eating seafood for years since then.

The angle of the sun hit the back of her neck at just the right spot, dousing her in a slice of warmth even though there was a bit of a chill in the air.

The sun in Verona had been warm, not too intense, but wonderful to bask in. But here in Venice there was a bite to the air, but she had been prepared and had worn her cream woolen dress, with brown woolen tights, leather boots and a tight-fitting leather jacket over it. She was warm, and she was content. She would survive.

She would return to Denver shortly and carry on with her life just as it had been before she left. Over time Nico and Verona would slowly disappear from her memories. Concentrating on her online store would be a good distraction. She would build it up so that it was better than ever, and she would find new ways of attracting customers.

She would never go back to copywriting again. She had managed to make do so far without the writing assignments, and she hadn't worked at all during the time she had been in Italy.

The income from her online site was just about bringing in enough to tide her over. She dared to imagine the possibilities if she doubled, tripled or quadrupled her income. The idea excited her. It was possible, especially if she added Andrea's products to the mix. She'd only been to Montova once, but she could call Andrea and organize some sort of bulk purchase. And then, with new products, her income could only increase. Of course, she would have to figure out shipment costs, but anything was possible.

A server delivered a warm chocolate croissant to the table behind her, passing directly in Ava's line of vision and leaving her craving one for herself, to go along with the delicious panino. Just at that moment an image of her and Nico eating panini by the stream flashed in front of her.

No matter how hard she tried to forget him, he was always in her thoughts. Whenever she remembered him, she remembered their kiss. In truth, she had thought of nothing else but that kiss during the entire train journey to Venice.

She bit into her panino and regarded the irony of her situation. Here she was taking her vacation in Italy, in a bid to get away from the disaster of being jilted six weeks before her wedding day. And now that she was in Italy, she found herself embroiled in yet another disastrous situation.

Despite her best efforts she had started to develop feelings for a man who had, it seemed, turned out to be a liar and a cheat.

And a father, too.

*How bad could it get?*

Nobody needed to ever know about her little summer romance that died before it had even had a chance to start up. She would never mention this non-event to anyone.

She put her unfinished panino down on the plate, and looked around, her attention riveted to a magazine rack close by at a kiosk. The scarlet red dress on the fashion model on the cover of *Italian Vogue* caught her eye.

She wondered whether she should get up to buy the magazine after she had finished her coffee, or whether she should get up now and buy it, leaving her coffee cup temporarily unattended at the table.

The magazine rack was only a stone's throw away. She looked around, wondering what she should do, then wondered why she was thinking so much about wondering what to do. Images of her and Nico kissing, and the hot feelings they aroused, left her unable to think straight about anything else.

It was then that her gaze fell upon a photo of Nico. It was

a close-up of his face, and it was on the front cover of an Italian newspaper.

What was he doing on the front cover of a newspaper?

She got up slowly from her table, her eyes fixed on the black and white newspaper so snugly embedded in the newspaper stand. She walked toward it stealthily, then picked it up and unfolded it. There he was—those dark eyes, even in black and white—were so beautiful. The thick dark hair and that indisputably handsome face. Underneath the photo, the words: Nico Cazale and then something in Italian that she couldn't make out.

Her heart fluttered furiously as her eyes quickly skimmed the two columns of writing devoted to him. It was a business paper, so she didn't think it was any type of tabloid news. She scanned for the words "Silvia" and anything else that might be un-businesslike.

Anything that gave a hint of a marriage.

She wasn't interested in business news or mergers. She wanted to know about the human mergers such as marriage. Her eyes flitted speedily over the words, looking for the words she didn't want to find when all of a sudden, the words "Hello, Ava," sailed into her ears and knocked the wind right out of her.

She knew, in that instant, who it was.

Nico stepped out from behind the newspaper stand; all six-foot-two inches of him, in his business suit and crisp white shirt. Unlike the usual confident and self-assured Nico that she was used to, he now seemed a little unsure.

Ava stared back, not sure whether this was a dream or real. Nico in the newspaper and now in the flesh before her. Not in Verona, but here in Venice.

A million words and questions floated through her mind

and stayed trapped in her throat. But the only word that came out was, "*You?*"

It was all too much to take in too soon. She had only left him yesterday evening, when Silvia had taken a knife to her heart and dug right in. Now he turned up here, when she least expected to see him.

She dropped the newspaper, stepped towards him and raised her hand toward his face. An irrational urge to slap him suddenly consumed her, but she managed to rein in her anger. Instead, her hand remained suspended in mid-air, and she stared straight into Nico's pained eyes. Feeling foolish, she lowered her hand and looked away, unsure of her conflicting feelings for him.

Nico reached out to take her hand, but she stepped back, out of his reach. He watched her calmly. "You should have slapped me, if it would have made you feel better." There was still no expression on his face, no signs of anger, no smile. He continued watching her, then he picked up the newspaper that she had dropped, paid the kiosk owner and took her gently by the crook of her elbow. He led her back to her table.

His manner left her at a loss for words and so she complied. The burst of anger she had felt when she first saw him had disappeared as soon as she had looked into his eyes.

But now she had questions that needed to be answered. Why was he here? Where was Silvia? Where was his child?

"Have you been following me?" she asked angrily, shaking her arm away. She moved over to her side of the table and sat back down again. Her cappuccino was cold, and she pushed it away. Nico moved his chair from the opposite end of the white cast iron table and moved it alongside hers. He threw the newspaper onto the table and his picture stared back at them.

"I'm sorry." His eyes, so angry and cold yesterday were

now soft and warm. Ava looked at him and for a fleeting second, she felt a tinge of sadness, too. For him, for her. For their situation.

But the sadness quickly gave way to anger as her gaze fell onto his picture. "I was expecting to see a picture of your bride," she said with venom.

"My *bride*?" He looked genuinely surprised to hear this.

"You and Silvia; apparently you have a daughter together. Or was that some minor detail that you forgot to tell me? I'm assuming you're also married, or will be, at some point. That's your next secret, isn't it?" She was savage in the way she tossed these words at him so contemptuously. She crossed her arms tightly around her chest, and crossed her legs, too, staring at him with eyes that were cold.

The news temporarily stunned Nico into silence. She could tell he hadn't seen this one coming.

"Yeah, I figured you wouldn't know how to get out of it," she snarled.

"Hmmm." Nico snorted. "That's what she told you?"

Ava sneered at him. "You deny it then? Next, you'll be telling me that you're not really a playboy either."

Nico's face hardened. "I'm not. Maybe six or seven years ago I might have been a bit carefree about things. But I've changed a lot since then. I don't blame you for having that impression about me."

"When's the wedding?" Ava continued, at full speed.

"There is no wedding. There never was. We were never really a couple," Nico said firmly. "I can't ask you to believe me. I can't ask anything of you, Ava, I know that. But I'm telling you the truth now. I've never lied to you. There were times, I don't deny it, that I might not have told you certain things, but I never lied. I was wrong to hide things about my past. Don't believe Silvia's lies. We had the paternity test and it proves I'm not the father. Silvia and I haven't been together since that summer when my mother passed away."

Her heart filled to bursting, as if a little globe of sunshine nestled gently in her ribcage. She wanted to believe, so much, so desperately. She searched his eyes as if looking for confirmation.

Nico nodded. "It's true. Ask my father." He seemed desperate for her to hear his side of the story.

They sat at the table, together but apart. Nico's dark eyes glittered as he spoke. "Alessa is not mine. I always knew that, but Silvia kept telling everyone otherwise. It's possible that as the years went by she started to believe it herself. I decided to end these rumors. And my father, too, wanted to know." He said this to himself more than to her. "You met him that day."

Ava let out a mock peal of laughter, slowly uncrossing her arms and letting her hands splay out onto the table. "Ahhh, yes. Mr. Cazale. You did mention him to me, that your father was the owner of the hotel. All the pieces of the puzzle are starting to take shape. I knew there had been bits missing. If only I'd known this the other day, I might have made a play for your father instead of you, being the gold digger that you think I am."

She immediately regretted saying anything about his father, but the words had come out and it was too late to take them back.

Nico placed his hands on the table and leaned closer to Ava. "I'm sorry you felt deceived by my actions. I never intended to hurt you. You mentioned the watch, the suit, and then you kissed me. I've had that type of attention all my life. It's what I know and what I can see from a mile away and what I run away from. It's the reason why, when you mistook me for a driver from the hotel, I didn't correct you. I liked that you didn't see what most women see when they look at me.

The Cazale name, the money, the reputation and the prestige. You knew none of that and I liked that very much." His eyes pleaded for forgiveness, but Ava wasn't giving in so easily.

"You didn't fit the picture as someone who was just a driver for the hotel. And for what it's worth, I noticed your watch the first day we met. It's so damn big it would be hard not to. I noticed your expensive designer suits, too, and wondered how could a man who dressed like you and had your—how shall I put it—your presence—how could he be a mere driver? But I was too preoccupied with my own problems to think about it for too long. I didn't want your attention, Nico; don't you remember that? I wanted to be left alone. *You* were the one who hounded *me*. You offered to take me here and there. I was all set to visit Pisa and Milan until you convinced me to go to Montova. I didn't ask you to do these things for me. I only wanted to be left alone. I wanted this holiday to give me some peace. But you didn't let me have that peace."

It had all come rushing out, the words she had held inside for too long, and now they were all out and she didn't care what he thought. She sat upright in her chair placing her arms firmly against the armrests, as though she might slip down and onto the floor if she let go of them. She watched him, sitting in front of her looking downcast and she waited to hear what else he had to say.

Instead, Nico folded his hands together, interlocking his fingers. "I'm sorry I hurt you."

"That's it?" she cried. "I tell you my feelings in an attempt to explain to you that I wasn't the gold digger you had me down for and that's all you have to say in your defense. *Sorry?*"

Nico sat with his head bowed, taking the full brunt of her onslaught.

"You held me, we kissed, we—" she stopped, not wanting to tell him that she was starting to feel something for him. Would she have felt something for anyone who would have shown her kindness? Had Connor's blow been that severe? She wasn't sure anymore. If anything, she was more confused than ever.

That moment they kissed now clouded her judgment. It might not have meant anything to him, but the last thing she wanted him to know was that she had thought of nothing else.

Changing tactic, she said, "I have Silvia telling me that you have a child, telling me to stay away from you; I see you and your father and Silvia with a little girl." She fought for composure before adding in a whisper, "And all I could think of was how you had used me." She took a deep breath, more to still her emotions so she would not do the very thing she felt like doing—crumbling into pieces in front of him.

But as she glanced at him, Nico lifted his head; something she said must have inflamed him because his eyes were blazing once more. She had come to know his body signals well enough now to read his moods. It didn't look as if he was going to say anything anytime too soon.

She got ready for another assault. "I wasn't looking to meet anyone when I came here. Believe me when I tell you that men were the furthest things from my mind. The only reason I asked you that day by the stream, when we were in Montagnano, was because I thought we had a moment of closeness. I felt you were opening up to me. I wanted to know who you are. I knew you were keeping something from me. As it turns out, you were keeping a whole other side of your life from me. You used me, didn't you?"

He let out an angry gasp and waited before launching into his own explanation. "I was trying to make this a good holiday for you. I wasn't making a play for you. That wasn't my intention...though, it was hard to keep away from you. You were so different to the type of women I've come to know. And because you were here alone ... I felt a little sorry for you."

Ava shot forward in her chair and cocked her head towards him haughtily. "You felt sorry for me?" Her eyes narrowed as she waited for his response.

Nico opened his mouth and then closed it again, obviously having second thoughts about what he was going to say.

Ava countered, "Why would you feel sorry for me? Do I look that desperate to you? A woman alone on holiday? Do you really find it so hard to believe that a woman alone might actually want to be left alone?" Her voice was getting louder and people around them were starting to look their way.

"Let's take this discussion somewhere else shall we?" Nico suggested, anxious to take this public demonstration away from prying eyes and ears.

"Answer my question." She got up and moved away from him as though the mere proximity of him was objectionable to her.

Nico followed her cautiously, obviously not wanting to make an already bad situation even worse. A few strides were all it took for him to catch up with her, and when he did, he placed his hands lightly on her shoulders, gently forcing her to turn toward him. But Ava stared at him with such contempt that he released his hands and left them dangling by his sides.

"Why are you so mad at me?" A hint of irritation crept into his voice. "Why so much melodrama, Ava?" She could tell that he regretted the words as soon as he said them. He put a placating hand up, but it was too late to salvage the damage.

"You feel sorry for me?" she sneered again. "Was that

your pity you were giving me over by the bench at Montagnano? Is that what you tell all women who catch your eye?" She kept on pummeling him with her words and even though she knew this was a pointless conversation, she couldn't help herself.

She wanted to hurt him and make him feel as bad as she had felt yesterday. He looked so despondent, and she knew she should stop carrying on so, but each time he opened his mouth he said something else that set her off.

He stared at her pensively. She had seen that look on him before, when he wasn't quite sure whether he ought to say what was on his mind.

"Well, say it then." She glared at him as she stood in a confrontational pose before him.

Nico was silent again. He blinked, then looked away before throwing his hands up in the air and raising his eyes to hers. "I know something happened to you, but I don't know what."

Ava gulped. *Come again?*

"What?" she asked in a whisper. It was as if the wind had been knocked out of her lungs and she was gasping for air. Ava stared at him vacantly as thoughts clashed in her mind. What on earth was he talking about? When she didn't respond, he continued, "I could feel you were very sad, that first day at the airport when you landed."

Ava's eyes rolled upwards. She was thinking back to that day when she had arrived.

"My flight was delayed, and I lost my luggage. Big deal." She turned around and carried on walking.

Nico followed hard on her heels. "I'm not talking about that," he said softly. "I know this trip was meant to be your honeymoon."

For the second time, Ava stopped dead in her tracks. She

turned around and stared at him. "Life threw me a curveball," she said at last.

Nico stopped and looked at her, waiting for her to go on. She could tell by the puzzled expression on his face that he had no idea what had happened. Of course, he would have known that the hotel reservation had been made in both her and Connor's names, and yet he had never questioned her about Connor.

If she had been curious about him, he must have been as curious about her.

"I was a jilted bride," Ava said quietly.

Nico's face relaxed slightly, and then he shook his head. "I'm sorry to hear that."

"It's done. It happened. I came here to get over it."

"Gina saw your wedding ring and when you turned up without your husband, crying and looking so sad, well, she thought you were a widow."

"A widow? What a thing to think!" cried Ava, looking down at her ring. It was the ring that Rona had lent her to keep her safe from uninvited attention, but it had ended up causing a whole set of other problems altogether.

"I didn't quite believe that story," Nico admitted, his hands by his sides, watching her quietly. "But then again, I can't believe how anyone could leave you." His voice was soft.

She looked up again and examined Nico's face before calmly declaring, "My fiancé called off the wedding six weeks before we were due to get married. He said he couldn't go through with it. He told me he didn't love me anymore."

Nico was silent for the longest time. "The man is a fool. And a cruel one at that."

Pretending not to hear him Ava continued, "I cancelled everything: the wedding, the hotel, the food, the flowers, the dress. But I couldn't bring myself to cancel the honeymoon. I love Italy; I love everything about it. I had to get away. I needed time away from my friends and family. So, I decided to here alone."

"And so you did," Nico said softly, starting to move toward her slowly, but she gave him such a withering look that he stopped where he was.

"Then at the airport, I saw the hotel signs you were carrying and thought you were a driver from the hotel. I wasn't thinking straight. You took me to the hotel and then you were so nice and helpful, ordering clothes because I'd lost my luggage, taking me here and there, showing me Verona, Montova and Montagnano." He listened carefully, seeming to hang on to her every word and she found relief in finally telling her story. "But why didn't you tell me who you were the next morning?" she asked.

Nico took a step closer to her. "Would it have made any difference? You were here for a few days. Would it have mattered who I was? You were upset that first night when you landed. Even if it was because of your bad trip and losing your luggage, it didn't seem important to correct you. You thought I was the driver. How could I not drive you to the hotel? I'd just driven my father to the airport. I'd picked up the hotel signs that our manager had left there by mistake. In your fragile state it didn't seem important to put you straight."

"But why not tell me the next day? Why drive me everywhere and lie?"

"Because by then Gina had told me, wrongly it now turns out, that you were recently widowed, and this trip would have been your honeymoon. I saw your name and Connor's under the room booking. With only you turning up, I knew something had gone wrong, badly wrong. We wanted to make your trip as comfortable as possible, whatever your circumstances were."

"You pitied me?" she asked gruffly.

"I didn't think you needed any more problems in your way. I didn't mind taking you to Verona the next day and I thought nothing of dropping you off there and, if you remember correctly, I left you alone to visit Juliet's balcony. I had business to take care of and I was more than happy to wait for you. I didn't think you needed to know who I was."

Ava stared at him, lost for words. Then in a moment of madness she said, "I bet that's what you tell yourself each time a single young woman turns up at your hotel."

His jaw hardened and she knew her words had incensed him. She immediately regretted what she had said.

He was suddenly quiet and then he threw his hands up into the air in frustration.

"I never took you to be such a diva!" He stared at her in annoyance and shook his head. "I'm not sorry I ever met you. But I am sorry I came here to Venice looking for you."

These were the last things he said before he turned around and walked away across the piazza. He never looked back.

Ava's heart thudded as she watched Nico drift away. She could tell by his swift gait and his downturned head that he felt as wretched as she felt right now.

Why was she treating him so badly?

## CHAPTER TWENTY

Nico walked back to his hotel which was also the same one that Ava had checked into. Being in the hotel business had its advantages and being able to book into an exclusive hotel such as the Hotel Sant' Adelina at a moment's notice was definitely high up on the advantages list.

Opening the doors to the balcony, he gazed at the blue gray water of the Grand Canal under the orange dappled sky. This was Venice at its most beautiful. The famous city by the sea captured in so many films, photographed on so many postcards, and it looked the same: magical, vibrant and mystical.

He had to give it to them, Ava and her fiancé had chosen the two most beautiful parts of Italy for a honeymoon. Verona and Venice. He sighed loudly. What a shame their love story hadn't lived up to the expectations of the places they had chosen. He tapped his fingers on the edge of the balcony.

She was a jilted bride. She hadn't even been married in the first place.

He felt a sense of relief.

He couldn't fight his attraction to her, no matter how hard he had tried. The idea that she wasn't married, that she was somehow free, and single, made him feel better.

Where he had first believed she was not his to have, now everything had changed. Except he wasn't so sure she wanted him.

For him, their kiss had turned what had only been hopes and wishes until then into something that brimmed with promise.

At least for him, it had. But now their bickering was getting in the way. He tried to understand why she'd reacted as she had. When she had first arrived in Verona, Ava had been consumed by sadness but now the anger was starting to surface, too. If, as she claimed, she now felt used by him, it made sense that she would be angry with him.

But he wasn't the only one to blame. And he had never used her. He'd kissed her because he'd been unable to pull away.

Her ex-fiancé had ditched her. What sort of a man was he to dump a woman like Ava?

Too much had happened in too short a time, yet despite their wrong assumptions about one another, he still believed Ava was the most genuine woman he had ever met. She didn't know about his family wealth or who he was. She had gotten to know *him*, the real Nico Cazale. He had been, for most of their short time together, just a normal hotel driver to her.

*Did it have to end like this?*

At least he had tried. He'd come after her to Venice because of that same, strange attraction which he'd felt since the first time he'd set eyes on her.

He had to find out her story. He'd needed to know, before she walked away forever. And he wasn't so sure that he was ready to have her leave his life either.

Remembering the feel of her soft skin and her warm, moist lips made his heart beat faster. He felt a stirring deep in his core as he recalled how close to impossible it had been for him to pull away.

In wanting to make this a happy holiday for Ava, he had succeeded in doing the exact opposite. And it had all been his fault. Not only had he hurt her, but he had also gotten her embroiled in the problems with Silvia.

*Way to go Nico,* he thought miserably.

He would be sorry to see Ava go. He wondered how long he would have to wait to meet another woman who would see the real Nico instead of his wealth and his inheritance.

At least he had straightened things out and she was now aware of the real story. He would leave for Verona tomorrow morning knowing that he had tried to put things right.

The sun had cast her silken glow over Venice again, as she normally did at this time of the year, when Nico checked out of the Hotel Sant' Adelina the next morning.

He decided to have one last cup of espresso in the Piazza San Marco before catching the noon train to Verona. Before he checked out, Nico handed a small package over to the clerk in reception, asking the man to give it to Ava Ramirez.

---

Ava hadn't slept well at all.

It had been as bad a night as the night Connor had dumped her. Back then, she had alternated between moments where it had all seemed a dream and then she wondered whether it was real.

It was the same now. Only it was a different man. After four hours of tossing and turning, Ava hadn't been able to fathom what was real and what was not. She replayed the argument with Nico over and over in her head.

She thought about all the times he had gone out of his way to do things for her; the small ways in which he had tried to make her trip pleasant.

A shiver slid down her spine and the hairs on her arms stood up as she recalled their brief moment of passion by the bench. Theirs was a kiss that promised the allure of deeper things. She knew that as surely as she felt his strong hands caressing her face when he had kissed her.

The thought of what could have been churned her insides and set her heart racing.

She needed to see him. She couldn't return to Denver leaving things as they were.

She leapt out of bed, showering up and getting dressed as fast as she could. She flew out of her room and headed downstairs.

Where would she find him? She didn't even know where he was staying.

The queasiness in her stomach increased as she realized that she might never see him again and that he might already have taken the next train to Verona. For a moment the world around her seemed empty.

She couldn't let him leave, knowing that he was still angry with her.

"Ms. Ramirez?" The hotel desk clerk walked up behind her. "Ms. Ramirez, a gentleman left this package for you early this morning." He handed Ava a medium-sized brown, boxy envelope. Ava smiled at him before peeking inside. She pulled out the small black box, no bigger than the palm of her hand and walked to the large sofa nearby and sat down. Her hands were shaking uncontrollably as she opened it.

Inside, nestling against a backdrop of dark red velvet, was the beautiful bracelet that she had admired from the shop window in Montova. Her heart jumped. She gingerly ran her fingertips over the intricate beadwork and metal design. She picked it up and laid it out on the palm of her hand. It was breathtaking in its beauty.

She closed her fingers around it and pressed her clenched fist against her chest, taking a deep breath in as she held the bracelet against her thudding heart.

*He had remembered.*

When had Nico had the time to drive out to the village for this? Now she felt foolish as she thought of the things she had said to him yesterday. She had been in a foul mood when she had arrived in Venice. But now that the truth was out, things were not as bad as they had seemed. They shouldn't be parting as enemies.

Was there a chance that they could become something more?

Nico had explained his side of things, and it all made sense. As it was, he had his reasons for behaving the way he had. And he had only done it out of kindness for her.

Silvia, the child, his decision to allow her to think he was nothing more than a hotel driver, all of these things now slowly unraveled and the fog had cleared.

It was not too late to put things right.

She raced to the reception desk, with the bracelet dangling from between her fingers and the dark velvet box in the other hand.

"The man who left this for me," she said breathlessly, "did he say where he was going?"

"Madam, he checked out first thing this morning," the desk clerk replied, and then his gaze dropped to the bracelet that dangled from Ava's hands. "Ah. A Flamentagostini?" The excitement in his voice barely concealed. Ava remembered the name of the shop.

"Yes. Flamentagostini."

"Exquisite. Highly desirable, beautiful and very expensive, too. Be careful you don't lose that, Madam." The clerk was unable to take his eyes off the bracelet.

"But did he say where he was going?" asked Ava, anxious to find Nico before he left and completely ignoring the clerk's fascination with the bracelet.

"No, Madam. I'm afraid he didn't, but I don't think he can be too far."

"What makes you think that?" asked Ava, trying unsuccessfully to tie the bracelet around the wrist of her left hand.

"Because he would surely want to see your reaction after purchasing such a beautiful piece. Please, Madam, let me help you." At the nod of her head, the clerk gently fixed the clasp into place, securing the bracelet firmly around Ava's wrist. "May I?" he asked, looking up at Ava with great expectation. Ava nodded and the clerk ran his fingers gently over the bracelet.

"It's beautiful, isn't it?" asked Ava, as they both admired it in silence.

"Flamentagostinis are created uniquely. They usually cost upwards of a thousand euros. This one might be a great deal more, as you can see it has a lot of detailing and many stones. We see a lot of these pieces here, as you can imagine," he explained, casting his eyes around the hotel.

At the mention of that amount of money, Ava shot her hand away as though it had been touched by a blazing hot iron.

"In fact, Madam. Isn't that the gentleman in question?" The clerk looked over Ava's shoulder in the direction of the glass doors.

Ava turned around quickly and saw Nico taking huge strides toward the center of the piazza.

She ran out of the hotel, flinging the doors open and raced across the piazza, tottering on her nude-colored sling backs. When she was no more than a couple of meters away from him, Nico stopped and turned around.

"I'd recognize the sound of those footsteps anywhere." His voice was friendly though guarded. He watched Ava with suspicion, as though he wasn't sure what mood she would be in today.

"Nico," gasped Ava. She stopped yards away from him, clutching her hand to her chest. Her face was flushed and she was panting but trying hard to sound normal. She noted his stern expression, then followed the gaze of his eyes as he saw the shiny bracelet she was now wearing.

"Do you like it?" he asked, his face softening as he put down his bag and placed his hands on his hips. She wasn't sure but she thought she caught a glimpse of relief.

"Love it, Nico? Of course I love it. It's beautiful. But I-I didn't expect you to buy it that day when I saw it in the shop."

Nico flicked his hands, as if dismissing her reaction. "I wanted to buy it. It is beautiful. Whenever I see a Flamentagostini now, I'll always think of you." His voice was low.

Ava moved nearer and held her arm out for him to see the bracelet. "But I can't accept this. I can't. It's too much. It wouldn't be right." She struggled to open the clasp with her free hand.

Nico watched her unsuccessfully trying to take it off

before gently grabbing hold of both her wrists. "I bought this for you Ava. I want you to have it."

The feel of his hands set her skin on fire and sent tingles of excitement shooting through her veins.

Not letting go, he said, "I came here looking for you because," he paused, and then his gaze dipped to her lips before he looked straight into her eyes once more, "because I'm not ready to have you walk out of my life. I don't want you to leave. We barely know each other, and yet at times I feel that you're all I've ever known."

She stood, frozen in place, hearing these sweet words that sent her all aflutter.

"Don't ever think I used you. You were never used. You were very much wanted. You *are* very much wanted."

Again, she couldn't speak. Her eyes were riveted to his face and her pulse raced. No man had ever said anything to her like this before. She didn't dare breathe.

Nico's expression saddened. "Now we know the truth, yours and mine, we can both go back to our lives, if that is what you want."

The somber tone of his voice shocked her to attention. Why did he sound as if he wouldn't be seeing her again?

"Don't say it like that," she said softly, "as though we'll not meet again." She felt drawn to him and wanted to inch closer so that their bodies touched, but he suddenly seemed distant.

"But we won't, will we?"

"Why not?" she asked, disappointment melting with sadness and sinking deep in her belly.

He raised his eyebrows slightly. "Why would we? When? Next year? Same time? Same place?" he asked, and she wasn't sure whether there was a tinge of sarcasm in his voice.

"You said you weren't ready to let me go?" Her voice was a whisper.

"I'm not. But I can't hold you here against your will."

"But we were..." Her voice trailed away.

"Good together?" he asked, finishing the sentence for her.

She looked up at him, catching the gleam in his eyes as he took a step towards her.

Embers sparked in her chest and hope returned as she held her breath, unable to speak.

"And that kiss," he continued, his voice low and husky all at once.

Ava blushed. "You remember it, too?"

"I will never forget it." He advanced toward her slowly.

"That's good."

"Good?"

"Because I remember only parts of it," she murmured, as her heart crashed against her ribcage.

Nico's face brightened, but she saw his jaw was still tight as he looked down at her.

"Just parts of it?" He had a glint in his eyes. They faced each other, inches apart. "Maybe I can help you to remember some more?"

Ava dared not answer. She wanted to remember this moment, in case, for whatever reason, she lost everything she had now. Standing so close to him that she could smell his cologne, her heart fluttered, and butterflies danced around in the base of her stomach.

Nico pulled her closer until she was against his chest. Without saying a word, he placed his free hand around the back of her head. Ava looked up into his eyes, so close now that she could see her reflection in them. She felt giddy and hopeless all at the same time as she willingly let herself go, falling against his chest until she felt his heart beating as fast as hers.

He tilted her face upward and the hairs on the back of her

neck stood up as he brought his lips down fully on hers. She lost herself in his kiss for an eternity, placing her hands on either side of his face and not wanting him to stop.

There, in the middle of the piazza, under the softly caressing sun, as people from all over the world strolled invisibly past them, Nico and Ava kissed and found each other again.

When at last she drew back to get some air, Nico said, "He must have been a very foolish man to let you go."

She moved her lips toward his again, hungry for the taste of him but before he pressed his lips against hers, he moved his mouth closer to her ear and murmured, "Because I don't intend to ever let you go now that I've finally found you."

Thank you for reading HONEYMOON FOR ONE! I hope you love Nico and Ava as much as I do. Their epic love story continues in HONEYMOON FOR THREE when someone from Ava's past turns up.

**Love, in Venice and Verona...**
Meeting the tall, dark and handsome Nico Cazale has turned her world around, but just when Ava thinks she can finally trust men again, a bigger problem threatens her new found love.

HONEYMOON FOR THREE is available everywhere

SIGN UP FOR MY NEWSLETTER to find out when new books release!
http://www.lilyzante.com/news

I appreciate your help in spreading the word, including telling a friend, and I would be grateful if you could leave a review on your favorite book site.

You can read an excerpt from HONEYMOON FOR THREE below.

Thank you and happy reading!
Lily

# EXCERPT FROM HONEYMOON FOR THREE

A slick sheen glistened all over Ava's naked body as she lay in bed, hot, sweaty and sated. She glanced over at Nico who lay asleep peacefully beside her. Just watching him sent her pulse racing.

He was beautiful. He had sought her out. And he was hers, for now. Whatever 'now' meant.

She had never expected to find herself in this situation: in bed with a man during her honeymoon. Not her solo honeymoon, for sure, and especially not with a man she had met only recently.

Yet even though she would never have entertained the idea of this happening, she could not deny having had wicked thoughts of Nico in the days before, right up until the end when she had fled the Casa Adriana, the hotel Nico's family owned, earlier than planned.

It had been one thing to have him rebuff her so coldly after their first, tender kiss. It had been quite another to find out, from a woman who obviously still loved him, that they had a child together. This was something that Nico had hidden from her completely.

Overcome by feelings of doubt and mistrust yet again, there was no way she could have stayed in Verona a moment longer.

Falling for the wrong man once was bad enough. She could not risk making the same mistake again.

But Nico had come after her. He knew he had a lot of explaining to do. Now that he had told her everything, she understood. The child wasn't his. Five years of accusations had plagued him and still he had said nothing. Then the paternity test had proved what he had known all along.

Her heart filled with warm love for this man who, until a few hours ago, she had been willing to turn her back on and never see again. Yet Nico was nothing like Connor.

No way. Connor was something else.

Her stomach clenched as memories of being dumped six weeks before her Valentine's Day wedding jumped back at her. Lying in her sumptuous bed at the Hotel Sant' Adelina in Venice, with the most gorgeous man beside her, softened the hurt a little.

This had been the whole point of coming to Italy on what would have been her honeymoon. She had come anyway, without the groom, needing time away to be by herself and to figure out, at the age of twenty-eight, what her future life direction would be.

Even though she had known for months that their relationship was floundering, when Connor ditched her, the pain had been raw. She'd still been in love with him, right through until the end. But maybe they would have ended up going their separate ways further down the line. It was better it had happened before she married him. Just as it was better that he had confessed about his one-night stand.

Feeling slightly cooler now, she wrapped the soft sheet around her and turned to her side to look at Nico. It was sometime in the afternoon, and they hadn't drawn the curtains when they had rushed in, desperate to feel each other in the flesh.

Golden light streamed in, casting a yellow haze everywhere and soaked Nico in a warm light. He slept so deeply, this beautiful, handsome man and she resisted the urge to run her hands over his face. But she could not resist letting her fingers dance lightly across his bare chest. He, too, lay on his side with his arm across her hip. She bent her head and kissed the big curve of his bicep, where it dipped slightly. Just the smell of him sent a warm fuzzy feeling through her body.

If things had gone according to plan, she would have been lying here with Connor. And now she had Nico instead.

He was everything that Connor was not and the stark difference between the two men in her recent love life was never more glaringly obvious to her than now.

A sudden clicking noise at the door jolted her. She flashed a glance over her shoulder, her eyes riveted as the doorknob turned. The hairs on the back of her neck bristled.

They had put out a 'Do Not Disturb' sign.

As she sat bolt upright in bed, her heart thumped wildly, and the figure of a man skulked into view.

"*Connor?*" She rubbed her eyes and blinked, then hugged the sheet closer to her chest. Beside her, Nico still lay asleep, completely oblivious to the intrusion.

Connor's gaze flew from Ava's face to the bare-chested man lying beside her. He slammed the door shut, set down his luggage and took a few steps toward her, his eyes swallowing up the intimate scene before him.

"What's this?" His voice was surprisingly calm, but he narrowed his eyes at her.

"What the *hell* are you doing here?" Her anger replaced embarrassment.

Now that he was no more than a foot away, she recoiled at his closeness, still paralyzed from the shock of seeing him, and having him see her in flagrante.

Not that she was doing anything wrong, technically. She was still single.

She watched Connor's gaze take in Nico's handsome face, his powerful bare chest, with its dusting of dark hairs. Connor's face reddened. It was perfectly obvious what she and this man had been up to.

"We're even now. Is that what this is about?" Not the words she was expecting to hear from him.

"We're *even*?" she snapped, incredulous. She wasn't sure what made her angrier, the fact that Nico could sleep like a baby despite the storm raging above his head, or the fact that Connor had the audacity to follow her to Venice and to turn up in her hotel room.

*I thought I had closed this chapter of my life forever.*

She was about to fling the sheet aside and bound out of bed before she remembered she was naked underneath.

It was hard to express anger while sitting in bed with no clothes on.

Nico stirred beside her; his arm still draped over her lower half as if he was claiming his territory. His slight movement caught Connor's eye. Outwardly he seemed calm, but Ava knew him too well. She knew that his unruffled exterior was only his corporate lawyer façade on display. As he flexed his fingers, Ava knew that inside he was anything but at ease.

"Yes," rasped Connor, looking at Nico who had only just opened his eyes. "We're even."

The sound of a man's voice in his hotel room shook Nico's

senses. He rubbed his eyes and sat up, placing his hand on Ava's arm.

"Who the hell are you?" he barked; his suspicious gaze hooked on Connor.

When Connor said nothing, Nico looked at Ava. "Ava?" But she had bunched her knees up and hugged them toward her, refusing to acknowledge his stare, or Connor's presence.

Connor held out his hand toward Nico, in a handshake gesture. "I'm her ex-fiancé, Connor Beachcroft. And you must be someone she picked up."

Nico slapped Connor's hand away. "Get out before I call security and have you thrown out," he growled. Connor backed away.

In all this Ava remained quiet, but her anger slowly bubbled away beneath the surface. Her mind was in chaos; confused thoughts married to disbelief.

What had possessed this man to fly across the Atlantic looking for her? Why now? Why at all? She needed answers but was not prepared to have a conversation with her ex while she and Nico were naked in bed.

"Go, Connor," she pleaded.

"We need to talk, Ava." Connor looked at her fixedly. She had never in a million years considered that he might come for her. She'd been broken when he'd dumped her and had done her best to continue with her life, putting on a brave face for the world when inside she was bruised and disappointed. Back then she'd waited and hoped he might want to talk and resolve matters and that perhaps he might even want to get back together again. But he hadn't even contacted her in the early days. It was as clear a sign as anything that things were over between them forever.

Now, after her whirlwind of a trip to Verona, and having met Nico, she felt as though she had been freed.

"There's nothing to talk about." Nico intervened; his powerfully built body naked as the sheet slipped even further below his waist. Connor's gaze wavered as he surveyed his opponent warily.

"This isn't about you," returned Connor quietly. "I'll be waiting downstairs, Ava. Just give me ten minutes. Please." He shot her a parting glance and walked toward the door slowly.

Nico had gotten up and put his boxers back on. He reached the door just as Connor did and let Connor take a good look at his powerful physique. He held the door wide open.

"Out, now." Nico's face darkened. He threw out Connor's luggage and locked the door behind him.

Ava sat motionless in bed, watching the standoff between the two men. They were like fighting cockerels, puffing their chests out and suspiciously assessing each other. She wished she had never set eyes on Connor again. The fact that he had walked in on her and Nico, invading the quiet tranquility of their world, had shattered her new peace.

Nico sat down beside her. "*That* was the shithead you were going to marry?" His hands tenderly grasped her arms, as he gently tried to unwrap them from around her knees.

The golden hue of their afternoon should have lifted her spirits, but she felt as if the world had ground to a halt. Energy seeped out of her body. "I don't know why he's here," she mumbled, more to herself, than to Nico.

He moved forward, slowly pushing her knees down and the sheet fell away, exposing her nakedness. He kissed her on the lips lightly. "It's obvious. He wants you back."

Ava hooked her arms around his neck and reeled him in closer to her. "He can dream on."

Nico rewarded her with a searing kiss that sent her senses

out of control. She kissed him back deeply, needing him all over again.

Connor could wait.

HONEYMOON FOR THREE is available everywhere

# BOOKLIST

**Honeymoon Series:** Take a roller-coaster journey of emotional highs and lows in this story of love and loss, family and relationships. When Ava is dumped six weeks before her Valentine's Day wedding, she has no idea of the life that awaits her in Italy.

Honeymoon for One
Honeymoon for Three
Honeymoon Blues
Honeymoon Bliss
Baby Steps
Honeymoon Series (Books 1-3)

**Italian Summer Series:** This is a spin-off from the Honeymoon Series. These books tell the stories of the secondary characters who first appeared in the Honeymoon Series. Nico and Ava also appear in these books.

It Takes Two
All That Glitters

Fool's Gold
Roman Encounter
November Sun
New Beginnings
Italian Summer Series (Books 1-4)

**The Billionaire's Love Story:** This is a Cinderella story with a touch of Jerry Maguire. What happens when the billionaire with too much money meets the single mom with too much heart?

The Promise (FREE)
The Gift, Book 1
The Gift, Book 2
The Gift, Book 3
The Gift, Boxed Set (Books 1, 2 & 3)
The Offer, Book 1
The Offer, Book 2
The Offer, Book 3
The Offer, Boxed Set (Books 1, 2 & 3)
The Vow, Book 1
The Vow, Book 2
The Vow, Book 3
The Vow, Boxed Set (Books 1, 2 & 3)

**Indecent Intentions:** This is a spin-off from The Billionaire's Love story. This 2-book set consists of 2 standalone stories about the billionaire's playboy brother. The 2nd story is about a wealthy nightclub owner who shuns relationships.

The Bet
The Hookup

Indecent Intentions 2-Book Set

**The Seven Sins:** A series of seven standalone romances based on the seven sins. Emotional, and angsty romances which are loosely connected.

Underdog (FREE prequel)
The Wrath of Eli
The Problem with Lust
The Lies of Pride
The Price of Inertia
The Other Side of Greed
The Seven Sins Books 1-3

**A Perfect Match Series:** This is a seven book series in which the first four books feature the same couple. High-flying corporate executive Nadine has no time for romance but her life takes a turn for the better when she meets Ethan, a sexy and struggling metal sculptor five years younger. He works as an escort in order to make the rent. Books 4-6 are standalone romances based on characters from the earlier books. The main couple, Ethan and Nadine, appear in all books:

Lost in Solo (prequel)
The Proposal
Heart Sync
A Leap of Faith
A Perfect Match Series Books 1-3
Misplaced Love
Reclaiming Love
Embracing Love
A Perfect Match Series (Books 4-6)

## Standalone Books:

Tomorrow Belongs to Us
Love Among the Ruins
Love Inc
An Unexpected Gift

# ABOUT THE AUTHOR

Lily Zante lives with her husband and three children somewhere near London, UK.

**Connect with Me**

I love hearing from you – so please don't be shy! Email me (lily@lilyzante.com), message me on Facebook or connect with me through these different platforms:

**Instagram | Facebook | Twitter | Website**

**Follow me on Bookbub**
**Follow me on Goodreads**
**Follow me on TikTok**
**Join my FB Reader Group**